The Magic Barber: An African Fantasy

A Novella

Tolu Adjapon

THUNDER
DRUMS
PRESS

The Magic Barber: An African Fantasy Copywrite © 2025 by Tolu Adjapon. All rights reserved. Printed on Demand Globally. No part of this book may be used or reproduced in any manner whatsoever without written permission and except in the case of brief quotations embodied in critical articles and reviews.

First Edition

Designed by Thunder Drums Press
Book Cover by @siennas.coverart
Names: Adjapon, Tolu, author
Title: The Magic Barber: An African Fantasy, a novella/ Tolu Adjapon
Description: First Edition. Thunder Drums Press

For Razak, my Barber

Chapter 1

The clash of steel rang out across the battlefield, rising above the chaotic roar of thousands of warriors colliding. Dust swirled beneath their feet as sandals pounded the earth, and formations slammed into one another with brutal force. The stench of blood and sweat clung so heavily to the air that even the circling carrion birds hesitated to descend, watching instead from a distance — waiting for it all to end.

The towering, relentless warriors of Kelenjara wore light armor and wielded deadly swords, curved axes, and broad spears. Their distinct diamond-shaped shields doubled as bludgeoning weapons, battering and sweeping aside anything in their path. They surged forward without mercy, crashing into the warriors of the Balansera Kingdom like an unstoppable tide.

Balansera's soldiers fought back with the desperation of men who knew the odds were against them. Their oval shields barely withstood the sheer force of the Kelenjara's blows. In the rear, some began to falter — trembling, casting anxious glances at their comrades. The front lines bent under the pressure, the formation threatening to buckle. Sensing their enemy's growing fear, the Kelenjara pressed harder.

Balla crouched beside the King of Balansera, hidden among tall grass atop a crescent-shaped hill overlooking the chaos. They watched as their warriors were pushed back, step by bloody step.

"Your Highness, they won't hold much longer," Balla urged. "You must send in my unit."

The king remained silent, his gaze fixed on the battlefield. Sweat and humidity soaked his thick beard. He placed a firm hand on Balla's shoulder.

"I know the time to reveal you is near. Yet I wonder... should we withdraw before our army is completely shattered? Perhaps provoking Kelenjara so soon was a mistake. We could have sourced our iron elsewhere. I know my family will suffer great losses if we bow to their tariffs, but maybe we should've tried diplomacy."

He hesitated, then added, "Your unit is untested, and you are few. If you fail, it may cost us everything."

Balla's jaw tightened. "That may be true, my king — but it doesn't change our reality. Returning the smuggled steel won't stop this battle now."

As if in answer, the rest of Kelenjara's reserves thundered onto the field. They hurled their lances high into the sky before charging in with massive, curved axes, flanking the Balansera forces. The screams of the dying mingled with the crack of shattered ribs and splintered spears. The enemy's pressure on the wings collapsed Balansera's flanks, forcing their center into a tightening crush.

"My king!" Balla pressed again.

The king's mouth twitched, and his fist clenched. His eyes darted across the unfolding disaster. They were past the point of no return. A retreat now would become a rout — and with no reinforcements left, nothing would stand between the enemy and the capital.

It was now or never. They would stand and fight, or their kingdom would be swept away into the savannah. "Balla," the king said, his voice heavy with finality. "There is nothing more I can do here. The rest is in your hands, and those of your anointed *barbed warriors*. I pray that these 'haircuts' from the barber Razak have the powers he claims."

Balla nodded grimly. He turned to the twenty warriors crouched behind him, hidden in the grass. "Ten warriors to each flank. We haven't had much time to train, but you know what must be done. Focus on the powers awakened within you and let go of everything else. Charge!"

Balla surged forward, leading his warriors toward the right flank. Thick braids whipped through the air from the tops of their heads to their shoulders, resembling a lion's mane. Lion paws were etched into the sides of their heads, near the temples. Their armor bore the image of lions, and the Golden Sun of Balansera gleamed brightly on their shields. When they charged, a primal cry echoed through the Balansera lines as the *barbed warriors* closed the distance. Was this the salvation they had been waiting for?

The *barbed warriors* collided with the enemy lines like an unstoppable avalanche. Balla and his men roared, their battle cries as fearsome as the roar of lions. The Kelenjara warriors staggered, taken aback as the deafening sound of lions' roars filled their ears. Disoriented, they struggled to regain their footing and regroup as they countered the onslaught.

The *barbed warriors*, with their lion's mane-like haircuts, cleaved through their enemies with terrifying efficiency. Their blows were devastating, overwhelming the Kelenjara warriors' defenses. On the left flank, a thunderous explosion of lightning surged through the ranks as a bolt of blue fire struck down hundreds of Kelenjara warriors in an instant. In the center, bolstered by the sudden fury of the *barbed warriors*, the Balansera soldiers rallied and charged with newfound ferocity. The Kelenjara army, now in disarray, broke apart and fled in panic, with the *barbed warriors* hot on their heels.

The Balansera Kingdom had clung to life by a single, fragile thread—and now, that thread was beginning to snap into victory.

The king stood, eyes fixed on the battlefield, watching as the army began to regroup. The *barbed warriors* were already lined up, standing in formation on the right flank. The losses were overwhelming. Out of the three thousand warriors who had been deployed, only nine hundred remained unscathed. Over a thousand were wounded, and the rest had fallen, slain on the field of battle. But despite the heavy toll, they had survived the clash with the Kelenjara Kingdom—the most formidable military power in the region, which had come with an army of four thousand. This was the enemy that had humiliated them for years, both on the battlefield and in the halls of diplomacy. Yet, for the first time, they had delivered a decisive blow to their hostile neighbors.

"Victory is ours," Balla said as he approached the king, his body covered in dust and blood. His sword remained slick and crimson with the evidence of battle. "Our powers made us unstoppable. Razak is truly blessed by the gods."

The king let out a long sigh. "Indeed. Victory is ours... but it was yours, Balla."

"My king." Balla and the other *barbed warriors* dropped to one knee in reverence.

"We have unlocked a new weapon, one that will shift the balance of power in the region." The king's gaze drifted beyond the battlefield, his eyes tracing the boundaries of Balansera's southeastern borders. "It has opened up new opportunities for us. But this secret... we must guard it with our lives. I fear that if we do not, it will bring us dangers we are not yet prepared to face."

Chapter 2

The rhythmic sound of steel sharpening echoed through the small wood-and-clay shop as the mid-morning sun streamed in. Razak hummed softly as he took one of his three-inch-long flat razor blades, its slight curve catching the light, and ran it across a polished whetstone. The blade glimmered, reflecting the early sun's rays across its sleek, smooth surface. Razak held it up for inspection, admiring the craftsmanship. His source for these uniquely forged blades might be an outcast, but the man was excellent at supplying Razak with exactly what he needed. It was ready now. He blew gently on it, as if extinguishing a flame, before placing it carefully on an altar at the back of his salon. He repeated the process with two other blades of varying sizes.

Once finished, Razak fetched a basin of fire-hardened clay filled with cool water and set it at the base of the altar. He took one of the blades and, with slow reverence, dipped it into the water, chanting as he did:

Diyaa ka faŋŋa la, kunŋo ka ɲumaa,
Fo n'danna la siraa ani baana.
Baaba ani naana ka n'nala yɛŋŋe,
Dunya kɛ n'kala ani tanŋaa yɛŋŋe.
Blade of power, edge of glory,
I prepare you for the path of destiny.
Fathers and mothers, guide its purpose,
May its cuts bring justice and strength.

Razak repeated the ritual for each blade, dipping them into the basin one by one. As each blade sank beneath the water, Razak caught his own reflection in its depths. His hair flowed in large dreadlocks that cascaded past his shoulders. His face bore a medium-thick beard and mustache. His dark skin had a subtle sheen, and his light brown eyes, sharp with focus, watched as he withdrew each blade. Rising from the water basin, he carried the blades to a wooden table when he heard a knock at the door.

"Razak! My barber, are you there?" A sweet voice called from the other side of the door.

Razak sighed and turned his head toward it. Not her again. "Yes, I know it's you, Fanta."

"Great!" The door flew open, and a young woman, draped in colorful beads and vibrant cloth, stepped inside. Her hair was intricately braided in tight circular patterns on the sides of her head, while the rest cascaded down her neck to just above her shoulders. She beamed at him as her dark eyes met his. "Oh, I missed your ceremony, didn't I?"

Razak shook his head, a small smile tugging at his lips. "It's just a small ritual to bless the tools of my trade."

"Ahhh, Razak, big man. Don't be so humble. You're the barber of barbers." Fanta approached and squinted at one of the blades. "These aren't simple tools, ooo, these are magical weapons."

"A secret not known to the rest of the kingdom." Razak gave her a pointed look. "My pet, sit still over there. I'm not done."

"Ah, really?" Fanta's eyes widened in surprise.

Razak took each of the blades, carefully dipping them into a small jar filled with oil, then wiping each one slowly with a white cloth.

"Ah, okay, my barber. So now these blades are ready for use?"

"That's correct, but there's one final step." Razak picked up the blades and placed them inside a polished ebony box. "I need to take them to the temple to have them blessed by the holy men. Then, they're ready to be used in barbing the next anointed warriors."

Fanta smiled brightly. "I'm always eager to learn as much as I can."

"Why? Do you want to be a barber yourself?" Razak raised an eyebrow, amused.

"Oh no, my barber. It's because of my upcoming wedding to one of your *barbed warriors*. My family wants me to learn as much as I can."

"Ah!" Razak stroked his beard thoughtfully. "So, the truth comes out at last. All this constant pestering and trying to learn my secrets. But why are you marrying one of my warriors?"

"Hmmm," Fanta said, a mischievous glint in her eyes. "My family says it will help strengthen our ties with key clans in the kingdom. Also, he's very cute and handsome. What more could I ask for?"

Razak chuckled and shook his head, gathering his sandals.

"I want to learn so that I can be of use to him," she added, skipping toward the table with the oils.

"I understand now," Razak said, a knowing look in his eyes. "But if you think you can maintain the haircuts... that, I'm not sure you can handle."

"Why not?" she asked, her curiosity piqued.

Razak fixed her with a steady gaze. "More goes into granting the warriors their powers than just the haircut styles."

Fanta leaned forward, her smile widening. "Tell me then!"

"Let's go," Razak said, gesturing for her to follow.

The two left the shop and made their way through the bustling streets of Sunjaro, the capital city. Merchants and traders hurried back and forth, coming from all corners of the region. Women, draped in vibrant cloths with intricate braids woven into their hair, passed by on their way to the markets. The sounds of children's laughter and play filled the air as they ventured deeper into the city's main roads. In the distance, the grand temple near the royal palace loomed, its towering spires reaching for the sky.

"My pet," Razak spoke quietly. "Everything I've taught you must remain secret. These people, they are the lifeblood of our kingdom. They go about their daily labor to keep everything running smoothly, unaware of the weight I bear."

"Mmm, interesting, Razak. Does this mean I'm one of the special ones now?" Fanta asked, a teasing note in her voice.

"Ha, don't flatter yourself." Razak smiled, giving her a playful nudge. "It's because of one of my special warriors' haircuts that I'm able to see clearly enough to tolerate your company."

"Really?" Fanta raised an eyebrow, pulling at the cloth draped around her shoulders as they arrived at the towering temple, its triangular spires cutting into the sky like great spears.

"Yes." Razak took her hand, leading her up the temple's grand stone steps. "He carries the hairstyle *Sɛruŋŋo Kano*."

"Watchful Eye?"

"Yes. It's a power that grants enhanced vision and perception, and for some individuals, it even allows glimpses of the future."

Fanta's mouth dropped open as they entered the temple. The structure was magnificent, crafted from stone, clay, and glittering precious gems. The holy men, draped in white cloths with gold-stitched edges, moved toward them with reverence.

Razak bowed and presented the ebony box containing the sacred razor blades to the chief of the holy men. The holy man took the box from him, turned, and carried it toward the altar, where he began to pray over the items.

As this unfolded, another holy man, hurriedly emerging from a side entrance, approached Razak and Fanta. "My lord," he said urgently, "The king requests your presence immediately."

Razak's eyes narrowed, his posture stiffening. "What's the matter?"

"The king has returned from battle. Your warriors have proven themselves," the holy man said, his voice serious. "And yet, the king fears we've unleashed something else as well."

Chapter 3

Razak and Fanta entered the throne room of the royal palace, the vast hall filled with the scent of ancient perfumes and sweet nectar. The polished white stone floors gleamed beneath their feet, and tall pillars adorned with intricate reliefs of the kingdom's warrior kings from centuries past stood like silent sentinels. At the far end of the room, the throne—made of polished ebony and studded with gold and rubies—held King Cissé. He was draped in rich silk that passed over one shoulder, with gold arm bracelets glinting on his arms and a gold chain hanging from his neck. His dark brown eyes were narrowed in focus as he gazed at Razak and Fanta, his brow furrowed with worry.

Beside the king stood Balla, one of the *barbed warriors*, and the beautiful Kandia, the king's cousin. The throne room was more crowded than usual, with an imposing table set before the throne. On it was a large, detailed map of the kingdom, surrounded by the borders of their neighboring realms. To the northeast lay the kingdom of Azemba, a wild and forested land. To the east was Senkoré, known for its fertile plains and agricultural wealth. But it was the southeastern region—the kingdom of Kelenjara—that held the king's focus. The map marked it clearly, an ever-present reminder of their savage, relentless enemy.

Razak stepped forward, bowing deeply before the king. "I came, my king, as soon as I received your summons."

King Cissé leaned forward in his throne, pulling at his beard, his expression grim. "Yes, you have brought new power to our kingdom, Razak. It is... impressive." He gestured toward Balla, standing to his side. "He led twenty of the other *barbed warriors* into battle. They manifested the powers you promised. Powers they didn't possess before."

Razak smiled, pride evident in his eyes. "And the result?"

Cissé's gaze hardened. "They turned the tide of a battle that should have been lost." He paused, his eyes lingering on Razak with deep worry. "But I fear it may be a curse rather than a blessing."

Razak's smile faltered. His brow furrowed as he looked at the king. "And this is cause for concern? Your highness, I thought you would welcome this news with celebration. Was this not the answer to your prayers? The victory you sought? Why do you appear troubled?"

Balla, standing nearby, glanced at the king and then back at Razak, his voice low. "The king is concerned, holy barber. He believes the victory was too complete. Too overwhelming."

Razak cocked his head, his dreads swaying slightly with the motion. "Too great? My king, it seems there is something more troubling you. What is it?" He felt Fanta shift beside him, sensing her discomfort.

The king rose from the throne, his steps slow and deliberate as he moved toward the great table. "It is exactly as you've said. This final battle was critical. To lose would have meant the fall of our kingdom." He placed a hand on the map, his fingers tracing the outlines of their lands. "But now, with the Kelenjara in retreat, something else weighs on my mind. We have won... and yet I fear we may have set in motion something we cannot control."

Kandia, standing to the king's side, spoke up, her voice tinged with a knowing smile. "Kelenjara will never forgive us for the smuggling operation, Razak. The one where we took their precious steel from under their noses." She chuckled softly, her dark brown eyes gleaming. "Their premium steel has been their pride and joy for far too long, and now we've got a piece of it."

"Yes, cousin." The king's voice grew sharper. "Your greedy scheme nearly cost the kingdom everything. The Kelenjara were ready to wipe us off the map for this slight."

Kandia laughed, her voice lilting and carefree as she joined the king at the table. "Cissé, my king, I've made us money. This was never just about steel. The monopoly they've kept on such a vital resource harms our farmers and our warriors, who rely on it to survive. What use is this kingdom if we are beholden to Kelenjara for everything?"

The king shot her a piercing look, his eyes narrowing. "If we are no longer here to enjoy it, what do we gain, Kandia?"

She smiled slyly, her eyes sparkling. "And yet now, my dear cousin, our kingdom is poised to gain everything. Thanks to me. And thanks to our holy barber." She motioned toward Razak, a playful grin on her lips.

All eyes turned to Razak, who blinked in surprise. "Please, explain," he said, his voice steady despite the growing tension in the room.

"Our king was initially skeptical when you came to our court months ago with your proposal to grant new powers to our warriors—connecting us to the very essence of our faith and ancestors through divine methods embedded in your craft as a barber," Kandia said, gesturing toward the kingdom of Kelenjara. "But trouble was already brewing. Regardless of my political schemes, Kelenjara was on the brink of invading us again. So, we reluctantly decided to give your methods a try. The victory we achieved exceeded all expectations."

"Things you didn't foresee, but I did," Razak replied, pointing to Balla's hairstyle. "*Dunfaŋŋo Kulo*, the Lion's Mane. Ten of your warriors, alongside Balla, were bestowed with the power of the lion. I styled their hair with thick braids that flowed back, while etching lion's claws into the sides of their heads to complete the *Dunfaŋŋo Kulo* style. They were imbued with fearlessness, unparalleled strength, and a voice capable of demoralizing the enemy."

Razak inspected Balla's hairstyle and cut. "How did it go, Balla?"

Balla nodded in acknowledgment. "As you foresaw, holy barber. On the battlefield, we were invincible. Our enemies fell before us like children."

Razak bared his teeth in a smile. "Excellent!" He then turned to the king and pointed at another warrior adorned with barbed styling. "For the other ten, I gave them the *Suŋkaani Fatta*, the Thunderstrike style. This granted them the power of lightning and thunder. I carved lightning bolts down the sides of their heads, extending to their necks, with a light taper and fade that amplified their power. With this, our enemies were rendered powerless. I'm not at all surprised by the outcome of the battle."

The king placed both hands firmly on the table. "And yet, you still refuse to reveal the source of this power?"

Razak shook his head solemnly.

"This is troubling," the king muttered, his brow furrowed.

"Forgive me, my king," Razak said gently. "I can bestow power, but I cannot explain how. Just as I cannot explain how the sun rises or why the plants grow, or how water nourishes the earth to produce food for man, I cannot explain the mechanism behind my ability to grant this power through my barbering. But I can do it. It is for your graces to decide how best to use what I offer."

"Which is why I want this to remain top-secret," the king said, pacing away from the table. "This is immense power, and there are more styles?"

"As you say, my king," Razak nodded. "There are eight other styles. The chosen ones who meet the necessary requirements may be granted these powers."

The king sighed heavily and turned to Kandia. "Do you see? Even more power. How are we to keep this secret? It will be impossible."

"Forgive me, my king," Balla interjected. "If the kingdom were to learn of this, would it not be a great blessing? This could be Balansera's opportunity to demonstrate its newfound strength. No longer would we be just a middle kingdom. Our enemies would have no choice but to respect us!"

The king turned to Balla, a deep sigh escaping him, his shoulders slumping as though burdened by an immense weight. His face tightened, his brow furrowing in concern. "Our enemies may grow more fearful of us. Kelenjara's grudge against us will not fade—it will harden into a relentless hatred. Their resolve to destroy us will solidify. The fear you speak of will only drive them to proceed more cautiously. They will seek out allies, turning our neighbors against us, branding us as dangerous monsters."

Balla's mouth fell open in shock, the words taking him completely by surprise.

Kandia nodded, her expression somber. "With the rumors of the battle spreading across the kingdom, it will not take long for them to reach Azemba, Senkoré, and beyond. Even the mighty Dakumbi may hear of it. We must act quickly to build strong alliances and secure our trade routes before Kelenjara can poison their perceptions of us."

"As you say, cousin," the king agreed, then turned his gaze back to Balla. "Do you understand now?"

Balla and the other warriors present nodded.

"We know our barber, Razak, is blessed by the ancestors, but the source of his powers remains unknown. That means there may be others like him in other kingdoms—or Razak may be unique, and therefore a target. Either way, we are venturing into the divine realm, stepping into the unknown as children learning to walk. We must be ready for the consequences."

The king then fixed his eyes on Razak. "Razak, can you barber the entire Balansera army? At least a force of fifteen thousand?"

Razak let out a low whistle, his eyes narrowing in thought. "Hmm, your highness," he chuckled. "Alright, no problem. You bring me the warriors, and I'll barb them. But, hmm... this will take some time. I'll also need to train a few other barbers to maintain the styles. These will need upkeep every two to three weeks, depending on the style. And there's something else I'll need to explore as well."

"What's that?" Kandia asked, her curiosity piqued.

"If I'm to barb the entire military, some of the nobility will inevitably be involved. However, when I first barbed them, they were unable to access the powers. I need to figure out why that is. I'll need more time to research this," Razak explained.

The king and Kandia exchanged a look of concern.

"How much time do you need?" Kandia asked.

Razak stroked his beard thoughtfully. "I'll need four months."

The king's eyes blazed with intensity. "You have two."

Chapter 4

Two months? Really?" Razak shook his head in frustration as he walked alongside Balla and Fanta, leaving the royal palace. "I have to train other barbers to maintain these sacred hairstyles while at the same time barber the whole army? All in two months? This is madness!"

"Hmmm, my barber. Hmm, it is well ooo," Fanta murmured as they made their way through the streets toward Sunjaro's market area. "Then you really should teach me how to barber, my dear."

"Barbering is a man's work," Razak replied. "It has been for hundreds of years. There's no telling what might happen if a woman attempts to perform this sacred barbering."

Fanta smiled, undeterred. "Yet my family sent me to learn from you anyway."

Razak returned her smile with a wry chuckle. "The money your family pays is good. But I fear you may be wasting your time. I'm not sure you'd be able to maintain the hair for your betrothed."

"It's a risk I'm willing to take," Fanta said, her smile bright. "Besides, I like it, and I'm a good hairdresser for my sisters and other relatives. If I can help them, why can't I help my fiancé? If it works, it helps us all, my barber. If not, at least I'll be a better hairdresser. Maybe even start my own business on the side."

Razak considered her words as they continued walking. She made some valid points. Perhaps he should reconsider his stance. "Balla, I'll be depending on you a lot."

"Yes, holy barber," Balla nodded. "Just as before, I will continue training the warriors after they've gained their powers. As you taught me, I will teach them control, the limits of their powers, and how to manage their strength."

"Good," Razak replied. "But don't forget the spiritual meditation and prayers to the ancestors. These powers are spiritual too. They must remember that."

"Yes, holy barber."

"Ugh, holy barber," Razak groaned, cringing. "It sounds so silly."

"I like it!" Fanta beamed. "Why don't you like it, my barber? I mean, my holy barber?"

"Oh, spare me, pet," Razak sighed as they arrived at their destination—the military academy where the training and barbering would take place. It was a large, rectangular one-story building, with a spacious courtyard and a field for assembly. Across the courtyard, a grand entrance stood, flanked by stone pillars leading to a great chamber with massive ebony doors. Inside the chamber, an ancestral shrine sat at the center, with an altar and workspace set up for barbering.

"I need a new name," Razak muttered, rubbing his beard thoughtfully. "Something simple and nice."

"As you say, holy bar—I mean..." Balla stuttered.

"I'll come up with something, don't worry," Fanta laughed.

They entered the main building of the academy and passed through the courtyard, where dozens of warriors trained with swords, spears, maces, and axes. Some sparred with each other, while others practiced their forms alone. A few were meditating beneath ancient sacred trees, focusing on their spiritual training. Razak surveyed the scene, pondering the heavy task ahead. The king's pressure on him was clear—something significant was happening. What if he couldn't complete the task in time? What would the consequences be?

Upon entering the main building, Razak turned to face his companions. "We don't have time, so I need your help."

Fanta and Balla sat cross-legged on the floor. "We are listening," Balla spoke.

Razak paced, gathering his thoughts. "First things first. Balla, I need you to assemble one thousand two hundred potential warriors for barbering. That's what I can manage in two months. I'll give you one week to get them here."

Balla and Fanta exchanged concerned glances.

"But the king said—"

"I know what the king said, Balla, but it's not possible," Razak interrupted, shaking his head. "I'm the only one who can work on their hair, and there's only so much I can do in two months. I can't even manage two thousand men."

"I see," Balla nodded, though his brow furrowed. "I will do as you command."

Razak turned to Fanta. "I actually need your help as well."

"How can I be of service, my barber?"

"Recruit twenty other barbers and bring them to me," Razak instructed. "You know my work, so you know the type of skills I require. I need barbers skilled in braids, fading, and etching. Gather them for a good cause. The expenses will be covered by my budget from the king. You also have one week to recruit them."

"I'm sure they'll come for free to learn at the feet of the master. Your generosity will not go unnoticed," Fanta said with a slight bow. "Master of all ways of head cuts." Her eyes sparkled. "In fact, that's what you should be called! For that is what you are!"

Razak raised an eyebrow. "Really, pet? What am I?"

Fanta smiled, narrowing her eyes with excitement. "You are Razak, the Headmaster!"

Over the next week, warriors arrived at the academy in droves, responding to Balla's call. His name was quickly becoming legendary across the kingdom. Every major province sent their strongest warriors to compete for the chance to become one of the elite *barbed warriors*—those who would be granted powers and play a vital role in the rise of the Balansera Kingdom. To even be considered, they had to meet Balla's strict criteria. They had to stand at least five feet and six fingers tall, be in peak physical condition, and pass an intense training test. Only after further evaluations would they be approved for the next stage of their training. Each regional chief handpicked one thousand warriors from their province, totaling five thousand warriors who arrived at the military academy.

The training began immediately, with Razak watching from his chamber. Balla wasted no time. He had the warriors run miles barefoot, crawl through dense vegetation littered with thorns, and jump over obstacles. Anyone showing signs of weakness was singled out for punishment until they quit, returning home in shame. By the end of the day, five hundred warriors had already dropped out. Balla made note of this, then sent the remaining recruits on a grueling run out of the city, all the way to the beach—half a day's journey away. Once there, they were forced to swim in the ocean's icy waters before making the return trip. Those who struggled in the water, or were slow to swim, faced additional punishment—more time spent in the freezing waves.

The following day, a new challenge was set up. The academy had been transformed with a complex obstacle course, built under the watchful eyes of Balla and his twenty *barbed warriors*. Massive rocks and wooden structures were spread out across a two-hundred-square-foot area. Dummy warriors were placed strategically to create an environment where the recruits had to think creatively and utilize the different weapons they encountered at various stations before moving on to the next challenge.

As the trials continued, two candidates stood out among the rest: Demba and Fadiga.

During the same week, Fanta took a different approach. Relying on her connections and the whispers circulating within the noble ladies' fashion circles, she began to track down the most sought-after barbers. These barbers were known for creating the most fashionable hairstyles for noblemen, styles that made their clients the heartthrobs of many ladies across the kingdom. Through this network, Fanta was able to locate twenty talented barbers—four from each of the kingdom's provinces. Her messages, carried by swift couriers, were promptly delivered, and the responses came just as quickly. By the seventh day, all twenty barbers had arrived at the military academy and presented themselves to Razak.

"Greetings, fellow barbers," Razak raised his hand to address them. "You are here because the king of Balansera has commanded an increase in the number of sacred barbers, and time is short. I'm the only one who can grant powers through ten unique haircuts and styles. While you cannot recreate these styles or grant the powers yourself, I can teach you how to maintain them so the powers stay with the warriors."

A murmur rippled through the group as the barbers exchanged wide-eyed glances.

"Any questions?" Razak's eyes scanned them all, his gaze steady.

"What do you call yourself?" one of the barbers asked.

A small smile tugged at Razak's lips. "Razak, the Headmaster."

"When do we begin?" another barber asked, eager.

"Immediately," Razak replied. "We don't have time to waste. There's one warrior who needs a line-up and a few other adjustments to maintain his haircut." He turned toward the entrance. "My pet, go fetch your betrothed, Samba."

"As you wish, my barber," Fanta said with a slight nod before leaving to retrieve the *barbed warrior*.

Moments later, Fanta returned with Samba. He was a muscular marvel, a warrior whose face held the kind of perfect symmetry that seemed almost sculpted by the gods. His strong jawline was accentuated by a light dusting of stubble. Thick, dark eyebrows arched over piercing light brown eyes, and his presence commanded respect. However, it was his hairstyle that immediately captured the attention of the recruited barbers. His curly hair at the top of his head had a wavy flow to it, while intricate, wavy patterns ran along the sides of his head.

Razak gestured to the ebony seat near the altar. "My new barbers, the style that this *barbed warrior* wears is called *Jiiya Kuu*, River's Flow. As you can see, this style has matured over the past three weeks." He gently took Samba's head, turning it from side to side to display the hairstyle. "When a *barbed warrior* comes to you like this, you need to perform a partial re-barb and touch-ups. If the hair becomes too overgrown, I will have to perform a full re-barb myself."

The barbers gathered closer, wonder lighting up their faces as they observed the warrior's hair.

"The razor blades I use are already purified and anointed. I will teach you how to do this with the blades I provide. Before you use them on the *barbed warrior*s, you must perform the ritual each morning. I've already done it, so now I will show you how I barb."

Razak opened the ebony box containing his razor blades and comb, then set to work on Samba's hair. With great precision, he trimmed the hair to the optimal level, reducing it to a quarter of one finger's length. Using his blade, he meticulously re-etched the wavy patterns along the sides and around the head. The intricate patterns resembled the flowing current of a river, weaving seamlessly from the top of the head to the sides and the back.

The barbers exchanged astonished glances, their gasps of awe filling the room.

When Razak finished, Samba's eyes flickered with a soft green and blue light, shimmering like water before fading away.

Razak smiled. "And now his powers have been recharged."

"Amazing!" the barbers exclaimed in unison. "We've never seen anything like this! Headmaster, we acknowledge you." They all bowed low in respect.

"Thank you, my barbers," Razak replied graciously. "I will teach you everything you need to know about performing touch-ups."

At that moment, a guard stepped into the chamber and bowed. "Forgive the interruption, Headmaster, but a messenger from the king has arrived for you. You are urgently needed at the council once again."

Chapter 5

Razak arrived alone at the royal palace and was escorted to a chamber, which featured a broad balcony overlooking the eastern expanse of the city. The room was stark, furnished only with simple cane chairs and reed rugs. In the center, a small wooden table sat, its unassuming presence a sharp contrast to the opulent throne room he had seen just a week ago. This was a deliberate choice. There had to be a reason they were meeting here.

Alone, Razak approached the balcony and gazed out over the city. To any onlooker, it would seem like just another typical day in Sunjaro. But something inside him stirred. His senses were sharper than usual, and the dormant powers within him seemed to pulse, slowly waking. A sense of unease washed over him—a premonition. He could feel it: something significant was coming.

"Razak, our holy barber." The voice came from behind him.

Razak turned, and the king entered, accompanied by the noblewoman Kandia. The king was dressed simply in brown cloth and leopard-spotted sandals, adorned with only a modest brown and white bead necklace. Kandia, too, wore modest attire—orange and brown cloth draped over one shoulder, with a red sash cinched at the waist.

"Welcome to the Chamber of Reflection," the king said, stepping onto the balcony beside Razak. "Here, serenity breeds the clarity needed to strategize amidst impending chaos."

Razak studied the king's composed expression, the calmness in his features belying the storm that simmered beneath. Kandia had seated herself on one of the chamber's couches.

"It is always an honor to serve, Your Highness," Razak replied, bowing his head slightly. "But if you've summoned me here, it suggests the matter at hand has escalated since our last meeting. I suspected this might happen, but not so soon."

"Exactly as you've said," the king agreed with a nod. His gaze swept across the horizon. "For the average merchant, it takes about a week to reach the borders with Senkoré on foot. For a company of warriors, just two days. Yet a rumor? A rumor can cover that distance in a single day."

Razak's brows lifted in surprise.

It's been over a week since the battle, and the whole of Senkoré—and beyond—has been set ablaze by the news of our *barbed warriors*." The king turned to him, his eyes burning with intensity. "The rumors spread faster, and the consequences have come sooner than we anticipated." He raised a hand to gesture to the chamber. "Please, come."

Razak followed the king back into the chamber, joining him and Kandia by the couches. It seemed that the moment for discussion had finally arrived.

"H-oly barber," Kandia nodded, a slight grin on her face. "Or should I address you as Headmaster now?"

Razak smiled wryly. "It's remarkable, Kandia. I only accepted that title a few days ago, and already you've heard of it."

"Like my cousin says, rumors spread faster than wildfire."

"Hmm." Razak stroked his beard thoughtfully. "Should I be worried then? If the news spreads that fast, we might have a security problem on our hands."

Kandia's smile was confident. "My eyes and ears are everywhere. I'm an asset, not a problem."

Razak's smile froze, his thoughts sharpening. That was something he needed to consider carefully, especially when it came to his outcast supplier. "Well then, my lady Kandia, Your Highness, how can I be of service?"

The king leaned forward, speaking in a low voice. "Kelenjara has been busy. They've begun raising a new army, and they've started sending emissaries to the other kingdoms—Senkoré and Azemba."

"Worse than that," Kandia interjected, "they're playing games with our traders. They've raised the price of steel produced in their kingdom, then sold the same steel to Azemba and Senkoré at an eighty percent discount."

Razak let out a low whistle. "They're trying to get attention. A move like this will definitely do that."

"Yes," Kandia replied, her fingers nervously twisting a handkerchief. "The immediate effect will be skyrocketing steel prices for us and the collapse of our markets outside the kingdom. I've invested heavily in these sectors, and if this continues, my business will crumble."

Razak nodded gravely. "They're using their monopoly to destroy us after they failed on the battlefield. But this doesn't sound like all they're up to."

Kandia shifted her gaze toward the balcony, her breathing slowing as she composed herself. "Yes, they invaded us to cripple our ability to export. But when that didn't succeed, they resorted to undercutting us. Now, with news of our *barbed warriors* reaching our neighbors, they're making their move."

"Headmaster," the king said, his voice low and tense, "they plan to convince the other kingdoms to form an alliance against us. If they succeed, we're finished."

"How so?" Razak's frown deepened.

"If they choose not to fight, they'll expel our traders and cut us off entirely. If they do decide to fight, they'll outnumber us four to one. We need the *barbed warrior* army now."

"My king," Razak leaned forward, his voice calm yet urgent. "We don't have the time to barber the entire army. First, not all the warriors are qualified. Second, even among those selected, I can only barber twelve hundred. The barbers we've chosen will only maintain the haircuts. But I am the only one who can anoint them and transform them into true *barbed warriors*."

The king sighed deeply and began pacing the room. "So, what do we do?"

"Cissé, if I may?" Kandia spoke without taking her eyes off Razak.

"Yes, Kandia," the king replied, gesturing for her to continue.

"If we can't prepare for war on a large scale, why not send the *barbed warriors* out in smaller numbers for reconnaissance and to disrupt Kelenjara's operations? That should buy us some time and give us a clearer picture of Kelenjara's ultimate plan."

Razak leaned back thoughtfully, considering the idea. It was an intriguing strategy—sending *barbed warriors* deep into enemy territory to carve a path for Balansera. He would need to employ a warrior with a haircut power he hadn't yet utilized, one suited for such a mission. Most likely, it would have to be one of the new recruits.

"I like it." The king settled back on the couch beside Kandia. "Headmaster, is this feasible?"

"Yes, Your Highness." Razak gave a small smile. "I'll select two recruits for this mission. One will be sent to Azemba, and the other to Senkoré. Azemba is a densely forested region, and their warriors are exceptional hunters, skilled with the bow. Senkoré, on the other hand, has both forests and vast plains. For the warriors scouting these kingdoms, I'll give them the *Sira Janta*, Forest's Canopy style."

The king and Kandia exchanged curious glances. "What power does this haircut provide?" the king asked.

Razak stroked his beard. "With this style, I braid the hair into intricate, vine-like patterns that cover the scalp, resembling a dense forest. This grants the *barbed warrior* heightened endurance and the ability to blend seamlessly with natural surroundings, becoming nearly invisible in forests or grasslands."

"Perfect." The king nodded approvingly.

"What actions do you want them to take?" Razak asked.

Kandia responded first. "They need to infiltrate enemy territory, uncover where the iron shipments are being sent, and, if possible, identify what weapons they may be moving. Also, they must gather any whispers and gossip from the courts. I'm not sure if they'll be able to get inside the palaces, but we need to know if there are any agreements or alliances that concern our interests. With this, we'll learn their plans and our options."

"Most importantly," the king added in a low voice, "they need to buy as much time for you as possible to complete your work. We need to barb as many warriors as we can. I've given you two months, but I'm not sure we even have that long. We won't know until we hear from the scouts."

Razak sighed. The weight of the situation was settling in. "How much time do the warriors have?"

"I don't want to set a hard deadline for their mission," the king said, his gaze hardening. "However, once they've gathered intel on the second priority—once they know what Azemba's and Senkoré's intentions are and how much time we have—they must return immediately and report."

"Understood." Razak nodded.

Kandia smiled. "We are counting on you, Headmaster."

An hour later, Razak was back at the military academy, deep in thought about his next move. He sat on an ebony bench, staring into the distance, as Fanta approached with a calabash of cool water.

"How did it go with the king, my barber?" Fanta asked, handing the calabash to him.

"Quite well, I believe," Razak replied. "But it means we need to speed up our actions. Please fetch Balla."

"As you wish, my barber." Fanta nodded and left the chamber, only to return moments later with the *barbed warrior* in tow.

"You called for me, Headmaster?" Balla bowed respectfully.

"Yes," Razak said, his gaze sharp. "The king has an urgent mission for us."

"Understood," Balla nodded. "What's the task?"

Razak outlined everything discussed with the king, including his meeting with Kandia, and emphasized the two key priorities for the mission. "We'll need two warriors for this."

Balla's expression soured. "Two warriors? That's one for each kingdom. It won't be enough."

"Don't underestimate these powers," Razak scoffed. "Two will be more than enough to slip in unnoticed."

Balla's brow furrowed. "Forgive me, Headmaster, but I must disagree. There's too much at stake. If something goes wrong, we'll need backup. At least two more warriors should be sent with them."

Razak scratched his head thoughtfully. "Fine, but that means more time spent barbering for me."

"I understand, Headmaster," Balla said, "but the risks must be weighed against the rewards. I know the king is pressing you on timing, but he carries the burden of the kingdom's safety.

We, however, are the sharp edge of the spear. We need to strike quickly, but also have contingency plans in place if things go awry."

Razak sighed heavily. "All right, Balla. What do you suggest?"

Balla unrolled a small map on the floor between them. "We'll deploy the warriors using the *Sira Janta* style for reconnaissance. They'll travel through the targeted kingdoms, marking key locations for meetings and reports on objects in the environment. The second warrior will follow their trail, ready to act should anything go wrong."

Razak smiled, his eyes gleaming. "A wise plan, Balla. We'll proceed as you suggest. What abilities do you recommend for the second team of *barbed warriors*?"

Balla studied the map for a moment before responding. "The second warriors must be just as stealthy, but also lethal. They should possess assassin-like abilities, enabling them to swiftly eliminate any threats."

Razak grinned, his lips curling into a mischievous smile. "I know exactly the right style for that. *Saŋko Fanta*—Serpent's Coil."

Chapter 6

Seydou rubbed his hands together in anticipation as he waited by the old well in the market. His mission was clear: meet with his disguised counterparts and relay the message from his king. All around him, traders moved about, and stalls filled with various goods lined the streets. Wheat, rice, millet, sorghum, and other grains were being hauled in droves by wooden carts pulled by donkeys—clear evidence of a bountiful harvest for the kingdom of Senkoré. The kingdom was truly blessed, but it could all be consumed by Balansera if this upstart kingdom, with its strange new powers, was not stopped.

Moments later, what Seydou had been waiting for appeared: two merchants pulling a donkey hitched to a cart loaded with firewood. The scent of the woods lingered around them, unmistakable. These men were clearly from the forests of

Azemba. Seydou turned away from the scene and lowered his bucket into the well. After a few moments, he pulled up the heavy iron pail, filled with several calabashes of water, and walked toward the merchants.

Their heads were wrapped in white turbans, their brown tunics and red cloths giving them an air of familiarity.

"Your donkey looks thirsty," Seydou said, offering the pail. "May I give it a drink?"

The two merchants exchanged a brief glance before nodding. Their dark eyes gleamed in the hot afternoon sun. Seydou handed over the water, watching the donkey drink deeply before guiding the men into a nearby market stall. The stall was tucked deep into the market, a clothing shop filled with hanging cloths, dresses, and garments. The thick fabrics draped along the walls offered ample cover as they sat cross-legged on the floor.

"Thank you for agreeing to meet with me, my lords," Seydou spoke, lowering his voice. "I apologize for the lack of hospitality. The sensitivity of this mission requires discretion."

"You need not apologize," Makan said, waving a hand dismissively. "We did not come to be entertained. We came to hear from you—what has happened, and what needs to be done about Balansera."

"I appreciate your understanding, Makan," Seydou replied. "The great general of Azemba is always welcome, as are you, General Jatoba, mighty son of Senkoré."

"We thank you," Makan nodded. "Now tell us—what news of Balansera and their powers? What demons have they unleashed upon the world?"

Seydou sighed and looked upward, his gaze heavy with the weight of the news. "It was a war we were winning—routing the enemy at every turn. The enemy's army of seven thousand had been reduced to just three thousand. We reached our objective: the river that runs between their capital and the trade routes to your markets, where they'd been smuggling our stolen steel at reduced prices. Securing that river would have cut off their supply lines, strangling them."

Makan listened intently, his expression unreadable, while Jatoba stroked his chin thoughtfully.

"At the battle, the enemy gave us more resistance than expected, but we were ready to crush them after weeks of relentless pursuit," Seydou continued. "Then, after suffering heavy losses, they committed their final reserves. We, too, committed our remaining forces, flanking them to finish them off once and for all. But we were deceived."

"What happened next?" Jatoba leaned forward, his eyes narrowing.

Seydou's face darkened. "Twenty warriors appeared from a hill in the enemy's rear, near the location of the king of Balansera's headquarters. Ten moved to each flank. I watched as they decimated our wings. Our left flank was paralyzed by a loud roar that sounded like lions, and our warriors were slaughtered by enemies moving with a speed and strength I'd never seen before. On the right, thunder rumbled, and lightning struck down hundreds of our men. The momentum shifted. Our king ordered a retreat. The war was lost."

Makan exhaled slowly, his expression grim. "These twenty warriors— we need to find out who they are and eliminate them."

"I suggest we capture them," Jatoba said, his voice firm. "We must uncover how they acquired these powers. If they managed it, perhaps we could find a way to acquire such abilities for ourselves."

"Such powers should not exist in this world," Makan muttered, shaking his head. "They go against the natural order. We must stamp them out before they spread beyond Balansera."

"Whatever the case," Seydou interjected, "we don't have the luxury of waiting. Balansera will not sit idly after this victory. They'll move to expand their borders."

"Why?" Jatoba asked, a skeptical edge to his voice. "Their grievances are with you, not us. Why would they start trouble with us?"

"A fair question," Seydou said, tapping the floor with his finger. "But think of it this way: Once they finish with us, they'll come after you next. If we fall, who will stop them?"

Makan and Jatoba exchanged a look of quiet concern. Seydou was right, but neither of them was eager to escalate the situation into open conflict. While Balansera's traders were already aggressively operating in their markets, their actions had been economically hostile, not politically so. But with these new powers at play, everything had changed. Security in the region would no longer be guaranteed by conventional means.

Anyway, my lords, I did not summon you here to recount the battle you already know about. My account is merely from my perspective, and I'm sure you've heard many versions of it. The truth is, I already know the source of their powers." Seydou said.

Tell us!" Makan urged, leaning forward.

Seydou's eyes narrowed. "They get their powers through haircuts given by a particular barber. Each warrior is granted unique, unnatural powers tied to the specific style they receive." Seydou let the weight of his words sink in. "So, the source of their power is a barber. He's the target."

Makan and Jatoba stared at him, shock spreading across their faces.

"How do you know this?" Makan finally asked.

"We have a spy in their court," Seydou smirked. "All the information we've gathered... it'll turn your thoughts upside down. And I promise you, sitting back and doing nothing is not an option. You're right, the barber is the target, and the king has already ordered the barbering of their entire army."

"Their entire army?" Jatoba gasped. "How many?"

Seydou rubbed the back of his neck. "They're aiming for... five thousand."

"Five thousand!" Jatoba spun toward Makan. "They routed Kelenjara with just twenty special warriors. We don't stand a chance against even one thousand. They want to empower an army of five thousand?"

A heavy dread filled Makan's eyes. "I see now why you called us here, Seydou. We must strike them now before they overwhelm us with an army of supernatural warriors."

"Exactly," Seydou's eyes burned with urgency. "We must unite our forces, invade Balansera, and crush them before it's too late. We will need a large force—twenty-one thousand strong. Seven thousand from each of us."

Makan nodded at the proposal. "But it will take time to muster such a force. Also, how do we counter these warriors on the battlefield? Even with numbers like ours, it would take all our skills as generals to outmaneuver an enemy whose powers we don't fully understand."

Seydou nodded. "That's why, when we invade, we need a handpicked group of elite warriors to locate the barber and either kill or capture him."

"I prefer we kill him," Makan murmured, his voice low and resolute.

"I say we take him alive," Jatoba countered firmly.

"Either way works," Seydou said, placing his hands on both of their shoulders. "Without the barber, they won't be able to create any more of these warriors."

Makan and Jatoba nodded in agreement.

"We will return to our courts and report to our kings. With our counsel, we should be able to move our kingdoms into preparation for war," Makan stood up, Jatoba following his lead.

"How long will it take you to mobilize?" Seydou asked.

"At least three to four weeks," Makan said, raising his chin.

"Same," Jatoba nodded. "I think we should each send our teams to capture the barber."

"Kelenjara will insist the barber be handed over to them," Seydou gritted his teeth. "We would appreciate it if your kingdoms would agree to let us have him."

"On that, I cannot promise," Makan said with a smile. "We are united on all fronts, except that one."

Seydou stared at him in disbelief.

"Sorry, Seydou," Jatoba said apologetically, "but my king would want the barber for himself. And it seems we all have different objectives when it comes to what to do with him."

Seydou shook his head, the weight of the situation pressing down on him. This would start more trouble than he anticipated. They were united in their goal to invade Balansera and eliminate the immediate threat, but the barber could become the root of chaos. Former allies could easily turn into enemies in the scramble for control over the barber's powers. This was a headache waiting to happen. Maybe Makan was right: they should simply kill the barber, and with him, the powers that came with him should be eradicated from this world. But Seydou had long served in the court of kings and knew better than anyone that kings rarely passed up the chance for greater power and glory.

"My lords, let's leave this matter for another time. For now, are we in agreement for war?"

"Yes!" Makan and Jatoba murmured fiercely.

Chapter 7

Demba twirled his wooden training sword as his opponent, Fadiga, circled him. A smirk danced on Fadiga's face, revealing a small dimple in his cheek. This was the final challenge, the one that would determine whether Demba was selected as one of the *barbed warriors*. The only thing standing in his way was this cocky fool.

Demba feinted a charge to the left, then spun right, swinging his sword in an overhead arc. Fadiga caught the strike and countered with a low cut, slashing at Demba's left side, forcing him to retreat. The air was filled with the ringing of blades as Fadiga unleashed a flurry of blows, his eyes alight with excitement. Demba danced back, ducking under some and parrying others, narrowly avoiding the attacks. For the blows Fadiga missed, he continued his relentless assault, twirling his sword in fluid, circular arcs, barely giving Demba time to breathe.

Demba leaned back, keeping his movements tight, waiting for the moment to shift the momentum. Soon, Fadiga began to slow down. There! Demba focused his gaze, then struck like lightning, aiming for Fadiga's chest, just below his neck. Fadiga moved like a blur. He shifted right, seized Demba's wrist, and pulled him forward. As Demba's sword dashed past Fadiga's face, Fadiga swung his sword in the opposite direction, spinning Demba around. Demba gritted his teeth, feeling Fadiga's blade press against his neck. He stopped immediately.

"Looks like I got you, Dem," Fadiga said, cocking his head to the side, panting heavily.

"Is that right?" Demba smirked, struggling to catch his breath.

Fadiga glanced down. Demba's sword was pressed against his side. "Not bad, Dem. You actually managed to make this interesting. Unlike the others," Fadiga said, his eyes drifting to the other recruits sprawled on the ground, exhausted after Fadiga had thoroughly thrashed them.

"Well done!" Balla's voice rang across the courtyard. The veteran *barbed warrior* approached, followed by attendants carrying scrolls, jotting down notes. "You two are the finest warriors of this class. You remind me of my time training against Samba. We were also the final two during our test."

Fadiga lowered his sword as Balla approached. "Final two? What does that mean? Did we make it?"

Demba lowered his sword, glancing at Balla expectantly.

"Make it?" Balla raised an eyebrow, a glint of amusement dancing in his eyes. "You two are the top of your class. Not only did you make it, but you will join the elite *barbed warrior*s."

It took a moment for Balla's words to sink in. Fadiga and Demba exchanged a look. Then they both roared in unison, raising their fists to the sky. "Ayo! N'faata!" they shouted. "Yes, we've done it!"

"Yes," Balla said with a nod. "Now you will go through graduation. Prepare yourself for the next step."

The graduation ceremony was a grand spectacle. Balansera warriors lined the path leading up to the great temple steps. Behind them, the crowd cheered as the one hundred newly graduated recruits marched in perfect step. Demba and Fadiga moved side by side, their formation steady as their unit marched down the paved streets of Sunjaro. They were bare-chested, wearing only a white cloth wrapped around their waists, extending down to their upper thighs. A gold cord was fastened tightly around their waists, and their war sandals thudded against the ground, the sound reverberating through the city.

"The city really turned out for this?" Demba murmured, eyes wide. "It's hard to believe we're the best two out of our group."

"Yes, they did." Fadiga whispered back, a grin creeping across his face. "I can't wait to get my haircut. I just hope it's something that makes me look even better. Something to match my already good looks."

"Don't be ridiculous. It's the powers that matter, not how we look." Demba murmured, a smirk tugging at his lips.

"Yeah, sure, whatever, Dem." Fadiga cracked a small smile. "I'm just looking forward to the fight. I just hope I don't get powers that make it too easy."

"I hope you get your wish, brother." Demba smiled. He was so happy that he could tolerate Fadiga's cockiness, at least for today.

They arrived at the temple and ascended the stone steps until they reached the entrance. The heavy ebony doors were swung open for the ceremony. They entered and proceeded into the heart of the temple, where they were brought forward one by one to the altar by the holy men. Prayers were offered to the ancestors and the gods of the state before each warrior was anointed with sacred oil, which was spread over their foreheads. After the blessing, they were presented to the gathered crowd, who cheered loudly as the kingdom now had one hundred new warriors—each of them poised to become barbed.

Demba sat nervously before the altar in the Headmaster's chamber at the military academy. Around twenty other barbers sat in a semi-circle, all fixated on the scene unfolding before them. A young woman in colorful cloth sat in a corner, scribbling on a scroll. Demba had already completed all the rituals; now, the final moment had arrived. He watched as the Headmaster approached, holding one of his special blades. It gleamed like clear ice in the dim light.

"Greetings, young warrior. What is your name?" The Headmaster asked, his voice steady.

"Demba, Headmaster," he replied, his voice betraying a slight tremor.

"Alright, Demba, welcome. Based on your training and our immediate needs, I will give you the *Sira Janta*—the Forest's Canopy Style haircut. This will grant you the ability to blend with the environment, whether in the forest or the grasslands."

Demba's eyes widened, and his throat tightened. He swallowed hard as beads of sweat formed on his brow. "Thank you, Headmaster," he managed, trying to steady his breathing.

He sat up straighter as the Headmaster began his work. With precision, the Headmaster used the blade to perform a "line-up," trimming the edges of Demba's hairline until it was neat and sharp. Then, the real work began. Demba felt his hair tugged as the Headmaster skillfully braided it. The braids cascaded down to the level of his ears, but the style was far from finished. Taking half of the braids, the Headmaster wove them together, forming a canopy over the top of Demba's head. The rest of the braids flowed down around the sides, framing his face.

Finally, the Headmaster took his blade and performed a delicate touch-up at the back of Demba's scalp.

Suddenly, Demba felt a rush of energy surge through his body—an electrifying sensation unlike anything he had experienced. His eyes flared with a green glow, his vision now as if pierced by green lightning. A hum of power resonated within him, making every fiber of his being vibrate with new strength.

Before he fully comprehended what had happened, it was over.

"Congratulations." The Headmaster spoke, turning Demba around to inspect his work. "You are now a *barbed warrior.*"

Demba waited in the courtyard with the other *barbed warrior*s. Hours had passed since his haircut had been completed, and he was practically buzzing with excitement. He felt like a new man! Under the watchful eyes of Balla and the other senior *barbed warrior*s, he learned how to manage his newfound powers in the academy's gardens. He could truly blend into his surroundings, whether it was the thick grass or the varied vegetation. There were limitations, though—his powers didn't manifest in urban environments, and it was likely they wouldn't work in a desert either. But none of that mattered. What he had received was more than he had ever hoped for.

Now, he was just waiting to see what kind of powers Fadiga had been granted.

Demba turned his gaze to the entrance of the military academy. "Ah, there he comes." His eyes followed Fadiga as he emerged from the inner chambers and entered the courtyard.

Demba quickly rushed toward him. "Fadiga! Over here! What did you get?"

Fadiga walked toward him, his eyes gleaming, and his cocky grin more irritating than ever. "Hey Dem, I'm done."

Demba took a closer look, his eyebrows shooting up in surprise. "No way," he breathed. Fadiga had a sharp, neat line-up in the front, but it was the sides of his head that truly took Demba by surprise. Snake-like coils decorated both sides of his head, with the tails etched down to the back of his neck, meeting at the tips.

"Gods above!" Demba exclaimed. "What style is this?"

"Saŋko Fanta. Serpent's Coil." Fadiga narrowed his eyes with a small, self-satisfied grin. "My powers are quite dangerous, so my training was done in a very controlled space. Even now, I'm not allowed to spar with anyone until I've proven I can control them."

Demba's eyes went wide. This was huge. Fadiga was already probably the strongest warrior of their group, so it wasn't surprising that he was entrusted with such extraordinary powers. "Tell me—what are your abilities?"

"Saŋko Fanta," Fadiga replied. "It grants me enhanced agility and venomous strikes. I can deliver paralyzing blows with my hands or any weapon I wield. I also have the ability to move with sudden bursts of speed for a few seconds. And I'm already fast, so... you know what that means."

Demba's mouth dropped open. This power was dangerous indeed. Fadiga would essentially be a living weapon. "Does that mean you can kill with a single strike?"

"Not yet." Fadiga said coolly. "But my powers will grow with each touch-up. The day will come when I can kill with a single blow. For now, though, my powers cause paralysis. Eventually, the venom will become deadly. I was told that I'll need to control how I apply the venom—whether I kill or just stun with a strike depends on how I control the dosage."

"Wow! That's incredible! This is huge news."

"No, it's not." Fadiga scowled. "Now I can't beat your ass."

"Ha! Thank the gods that the ancestors have given me an easy pass," Demba laughed, shoving him playfully before quickly pulling back. "Oh, was that too much?"

Fadiga chuckled. "Oh no, not at all." He shoved Demba back with a grin. "That's not enough. I have to mentally release my powers. You're fine, Dem."

"Great to hear," Demba said, smiling.

Just then, Balla and Samba approached them.

"*Barbed warriors*!" Balla barked.

Demba and Fadiga snapped to attention. "Yes, General!" they both responded in unison.

"At ease." Balla motioned for them to relax. "We have a priority mission for you both. You're both heading to Azemba."

Chapter 8

Demba wiped the sweat from his forehead, contemplating his options. He was completely invisible to any potential spies or scouts, his powers keeping him hidden among the thick vegetation. Deep inside Azemba territory, he lay low to the ground, watching the observation outpost through the dense foliage. It was a turret-like structure, perched high in the trees, guarding the path to one of Azemba's major trading towns.

He considered his options carefully. He could use the *Sira Janta* powers to slip by unseen, but leaving the outpost behind could be a risk. Fadiga, trailing behind him, would not be able to make the same escape unnoticed. Alternatively, he could take a different route, avoiding the outpost entirely—but that would waste valuable time. And if he decided to eliminate the guards, it would draw attention. The last thing they needed was to be discovered. However, the guards could also serve as an obstacle if they had to retreat quickly. Their presence could either slow them down or block their escape.

Demba sighed, still undecided. Both options carried significant risks, but he couldn't act impulsively. He pulled back into the underbrush, retreating further into the safety of the forest. His first use of his powers on this mission had been successful. He could blend seamlessly with the vegetation, merging his body with the forest itself. He'd planned to use his abilities during the day and refrain from doing so at night, when they weren't needed. The limitations of the haircut powers were still unknown; they seemed to vary depending on the user. Demba had decided to play it safe and avoid overusing them.

The mission was clear: gather information from the town and report back to Balansera. He needed to maintain stealth above all else. Eliminating the sentries was not necessary. He would focus on his reconnaissance and keep a low profile.

He moved deeper into the forest, using the thick foliage to mask his movements. Reaching a sturdy tree, he carved an arrow into the bark, pointing the direction he was heading. Beneath the arrow, he etched a symbol that would warn Fadiga about the presence of the watchtower in the trees. Once that was done, he advanced through the forest, leaving clues for Fadiga to follow.

Soon, Demba found himself near one of the main routes into the town. It was time to change his appearance. He retrieved a disguise from his leather bag and dressed like an Azemba game hunter. He buried his other gear in the earth, ensuring his true identity remained hidden, and proceeded to exit the forest. As he walked into the town, he reduced his powers, blending into the flow of hunters and traders entering the bustling settlement.

The town was alive with activity. Traders from neighboring kingdoms had come to resupply, and the market was filled with kola nuts, millet, and yam. The sounds of the town echoed—

blacksmiths hammered away at anvils, their forges glowing in the midday sun. This was where Demba's reconnaissance would begin. At the center of the town stood the local palace, with a temple attached to its side. The population was large—at least twenty thousand people—possibly with a war potential of around four thousand men.

Demba made his way through the crowded main market. It was clear this was a hunter's town—different game was displayed for sale, from antelope to grasscutter, even exotic zebra meat. But what caught his attention were the blacksmiths, their forges busy, shaping weapons. Curious, he moved in that direction, entering a shop already crowded with customers.

"Greetings," Demba said, raising a hand when the shop cleared for a moment.

The blacksmith, hard at work with a small coal forge, looked up, then returned to his work without much acknowledgment. "Yes, what can I do for you?"

"I was wondering if you had a supply of arrows."

"Arrows?" The blacksmith grunted. "What for?"

Demba blinked. "What for? For hunting, of course."

The blacksmith gave him a long, hard stare before returning to his forge. He hammered the lump of orange metal, then dipped it into a vat of oil. "Hunting? What's wrong with you? You should be asking for armor-piercing war arrows."

Demba's eyes widened. Could it be what he was thinking? Was this why there were so many supplies of game in town? Was this why the town seemed busier than usual?

"Haven't you been called up by now? If you're after arrows, you should be asking for the ones for the upcoming war."

Demba's mind raced. *War?* The pieces were falling into place. It was clear now that the town was preparing for something much larger than just trade.

"Of course, you're right," Demba replied, feigning understanding. "Hunting can wait."

The blacksmith nodded and disappeared into the back of the shop. He returned with a quiver of arrows. "Here's a standard quiver. I'll give it to you for four ounces of gold dust. Sound like a deal?"

Demba picked up one of the arrows, examining it closely. The craftsmanship was unmistakable—this was Kelenjara steel. The arrow was long, fletched with eagle feathers, and its steel tip gleamed in the light. The quality was exceptional.

"Your price is more than a bargain," Demba said, his voice low with surprise. "How can you afford it?"

The blacksmith paused for a moment, his eyes narrowing. "Have you been so busy hunting in the forest that you haven't noticed what's going on? Kelenjara steel has flooded the market at super cheap prices. Normally, before a war, the demand for arrows would drive prices up. But with all the blacksmiths trying to compete for business, the prices have dropped."

Demba's mind was spinning. This was bigger than he had imagined.

"That's most fascinating," Demba said, trying to keep his composure. "Where exactly are the supplies supposed to go?"

"The capital," the blacksmith replied, his tone matter-of-fact. "And you better get there within two weeks. Otherwise, General Makan will have you lashed. The war against the devils of Balansera won't be easy."

Demba furrowed his brow. *War against Balansera...* This was the information he had been looking for, but it came with an unsettling realization.

"Noted, thank you," Demba said with a forced smile, his mind still racing. "I'll take the quiver."

Demba made his way out of town, his senses still sharp as he retraced his steps toward the forest. But as he neared the edge of the settlement, a flicker of movement caught his eye. The blacksmith had stepped out of his shop, watching him intently. Demba's pulse quickened, but he didn't let his unease show. He picked up his pace, his mind racing. As he glanced back over his shoulder, he saw the blacksmith's frown—barely noticeable—before he disappeared back into the shop. *Not good.* He couldn't afford to be followed. Hopefully, it was nothing, just a fleeting suspicion.

Once he was deep enough into the forest, he focused on his powers. Drawing on the *Sira Janta*, he merged with the vegetation, blending into the surroundings like a shadow in the trees. The hours passed slowly as he made his way back to his designated position near the tree where he'd left his marker for Fadiga.

A twig snapped in the silence.

Demba spun around instinctively, his body coiling with readiness.

"No worries, Dem, it's me." Fadiga's voice rang out, causing Demba to relax.

"Ah, Fadiga." Demba exhaled, the tension leaving his body. "I didn't expect you to get here so quickly."

"Speed is one of my abilities," Fadiga said with a grin, stepping out from the undergrowth. "Surprised you're back so soon. I figured you'd take your time."

Demba reached into his bag and pulled out the quiver of arrows. "I was able to gather some important intel. Kelenjara is supplying the Azemba, and they're preparing for war. Makan is the general, and he's mobilizing the warriors for a full assault. They have two weeks to assemble their forces."

Fadiga's eyes narrowed, and he spat on the ground. "Snake venom! Two weeks? That's not much time. They'll be marching to our borders soon after. By the time we can muster enough forces... we might be too late. We need more time."

Demba nodded, his mind working through the possibilities. "That's true. So, we have two options. One, we head to the Azemba capital and get the full picture of what's going on. Or two, we stay in this area and sabotage their efforts as much as possible."

Fadiga smiled, a small curve at the corner of his lips. "You already know what I prefer: option two."

Demba sighed, his eyes glinting with resignation. "I figured you'd say that. But convince me. Why isn't option one the better choice?"

Fadiga dropped to the ground, picking up a stick and drawing shapes in the dirt. His movements were deliberate as he created a simple map of the region. "Let's say you're right, that Makan is assembling his army in two weeks. What do we expect to find at the capital? The same thing. Nothing will change, and your powers won't be as effective there—especially in a city."

Demba nodded, thinking carefully. Fadiga's logic made sense.

"But frustrating the enemy out here?" Fadiga's smile widened, the excitement in his eyes clear. "Now, that's something. Sabotaging their efforts, causing them to waste resources—making their warriors hesitate—it'll be both fun and a direct benefit to Balansera."

Demba paused, mulling it over. His gaze shifted to the quiver of arrows, the weight of the decision pressing on him. "Alright," he finally said, after a long pause. "Then we stay. We make them pay for every step they take."

Fadiga chuckled, his grin widening. "That's the spirit, Dem. I knew you'd come around."

Let's deal with these fools first." Fadiga pointed toward the guards stationed in the trees that Demba had carefully bypassed. "Afterward, we'll hit any other targets we can."

"I deliberately left them there so we could operate undetected," Demba replied, his voice tense. "If we attack now, the enemy will know we're here and they'll come after us before we can make a move."

Fadiga smirked, his tone taunting. "Don't tell me you're afraid to fight."

Demba rolled his eyes. "Seriously? Let's move."

They slipped away from the watch-out post and moved silently through the dense forest toward the eastern flank of the town. Along the way, they passed a group of a dozen young warriors marching along the path.

Demba signaled, his hand gesturing for Fadiga to flank them. Fadiga nodded, using a brief burst of power to accelerate ahead. Demba fell back, tailing the group from behind, his movements as quiet as the wind.

With a short sword drawn, Demba sprang from his cover, charging toward one of the Azemba warriors at the rear. The blade plunged into the man's back before he had time to react. The warrior let out a shriek, his body jerking as the blade slipped between his ribs. The others spun toward him, wide-eyed with shock. Demba ripped his blade free and backed away as they closed in. Their battle cries filled the air. In a flash, Demba darted into the forest, blending with the shadows.

"He disappeared!" one of the warriors sputtered. "Where did he go?"

Demba dropped to the ground, his breath steady as the warriors stumbled around him, pushing through branches and vines in a frantic search. The sound of rustling stopped when something dark caught their attention.

"There he is!" one warrior shouted, pointing.

They charged, crashing through the brush toward the lone figure standing with his back to them. His hair was etched with snakelike patterns —Fadiga. He turned with a predatory smirk, eyes blazing. In an instant, the blur of his movements was the only thing Demba could track. Fadiga moved like a storm, cutting down the warriors with devastating precision.

Some of them managed to stand for a moment before the venom took its toll, their bodies stiffening, gasping for breath. Others collapsed as Fadiga's blade found its mark, each strike swift and deadly. Demba watched in awe, his heart racing. Fadiga had taken out eleven warriors effortlessly. If they had ten like him, they could defeat a hundred.

Chapter 9

The king of Balansera stared at the map spread before him in the throne room, his breath steady as he forced himself to remain calm. For weeks, intelligence from reconnaissance teams had filtered in, confirming that both Azemba and Senkoré were mobilizing for war. Kelenjara had already begun its preparations, but that was nothing new. What was troubling, however, was the simultaneous movement of their other two neighbors. It could only mean one thing—a war that could bring an end to the Balansera kingdom. This was the regional response to the rise of Balansera's *barbed warriors*.

The king's gaze swept across the table, which surrounded by his generals, including Balla and five of his *barbed warriors*. Balla would play a pivotal role in planning the kingdom's defense. To his right, Kandia stood, her presence impossible to ignore. Dressed in a simple brown cloth over her left shoulder, with no jewelry around her neck, her eyes blazed with intensity.

"Your Highness," one of the generals spoke, breaking the silence. "We are ready. Shall we begin?"

The king took one final look at the figurines on the table, each one representing the varying strength of the kingdoms. "Yes, proceed, General. What are we facing?"

"Thank you, Your Highness." The general turned to the others gathered around the table. "Azemba, Senkoré, and Kelenjara have formed an alliance and will soon invade us."

The king's brow furrowed. "What is the size of their army?"

The general's eyes narrowed with concern. "The force is likely to exceed twenty thousand."

A murmur of unease rippled through the hall. Such a force was unprecedented.

The king turned to Balla. "How many *barbed warrior*s do we have? What has Razak prepared for us?"

Balla picked up a small figurine resembling a lion. "The Headmaster has five hundred *barbed warrior*s ready for you, Your Highness."

The king's eyes widened in disbelief. "Are you telling me we only have five hundred?"

"My king," Balla spoke softly but firmly. "It took only twenty to route Kelenjara, who outnumbered us nearly two to one. Now we have over five hundred. Such warriors are worth ten times their number."

"If that were the case, I wouldn't be so concerned," the king said, his voice rising. "But they're attacking with more than twenty thousand!"

"And this time, they know about the *barbed warrior*s," Kandia added, stepping forward. "Kelenjara is aware of what they can do. They'll likely prepare a strategy to neutralize them. We cannot afford to be complacent just because we have new powers. What we need is a plan to stop these armies before they reach our borders. Has the diplomatic route truly been closed to us?"

Balla shook his head. "If the reports from our scouts are accurate, there is much fear of us in both kingdoms. A significant amount of resources have been mobilized for this invasion. Even if they were to somehow seek a peace deal, any terms would surely drain us of every gold dust just to buy us time."

"Balla is right." The king stood up and turned toward his throne. "That window has closed. Our only option is to defend ourselves. But we must accept that our current crop of *barbed warriors* may not be enough."

"My king," Kandia approached him once he was seated on his throne. "We cannot rely on just five hundred *barbed warriors*. We need something more."

The king looked at her, his gaze heavy with the weight of his years, the lines in his face more pronounced than ever. "Balla!"

"Yes, my king!" Balla stepped forward.

The king leaned in. "The Headmaster once spoke of a special type of *barbed warrior*—one who could achieve greater power than ordinary warriors."

"I am aware of this," Balla responded.

The king continued, his voice measured. "But Razak has been unable to locate anyone capable of bearing that potential."

Balla was silent for a moment before responding. "The Headmaster did speak of such warriors. He said they would need to come from the noble lines of the kingdom. However, when he tried the haircuts on nobles, they did not manifest any powers."

Kandia rolled her eyes. "This isn't a question of 'if' he can. If such potential exists, we must try. My only question is how the Headmaster knows this? I don't doubt his abilities, but we don't even know how he acquires them... How can we be sure of his words when he doesn't know which noble can unlock this extra power?"

The king nodded slowly, his cousin's words hanging in the air. Silence filled the hall as everyone turned their attention to him. "Razak has never failed us, so I will trust him to deliver. But that said, we must develop our own strategy to deter the enemy and, if necessary, defeat them should they invade."

Razak studied his handiwork, the *Siri Sanno* style—Shadow Fade. This technique allowed the *barbed warrior* to disappear like a shadow at will. The gradient fade, from dark to bare skin, was punctuated by jagged lines, resembling fractures in the fabric of the warrior's skin. Razak stepped back, watching as the warrior's eyes flickered between white and dark energy before settling back to normal.

"Excellent," Razak said, admiring his work. "See, Fanta? Everything is progressing. We can still create the warriors we need, even if I have yet to produce the special *Tunka Barbed Warriors*."

Fanta paused, glancing up from her scroll. "Hmm," she hummed thoughtfully, scribbling. "We'll need them soon. With the invasion looming, we're far from his target of fifteen thousand warriors."

Razak turned to the warrior, who rose from his seat. "Be blessed, *barbed warrior*. Join your comrades."

"Thank you, Headmaster." The new warrior bowed before exiting the chamber.

Razak sighed deeply. "I know, Fanta. I know."

Fanta's gaze hardened, her lips tightening. "Do you honestly think that five hundred *barbed warriors* will be enough to defeat an army of twenty thousand?"

Razak's eyes softened as he turned to her. "I don't know. I'm worried, Fanta. I never expected this. I introduced the *barbed warriors* to save Balansera from certain defeat, but now I see—

this world won't give this power time to mature. Fear already grips it, and this is just the beginning."

Fanta's eyes flicked to the altar before returning to Razak, her expression growing pensive. "Where did these powers come from? Why do you have them?"

Razak exhaled, his voice heavy. "I never told the king of Balansera the truth. Why would I tell you?"

"Because I care about you, my barber," Fanta replied, her eyes glowing with an inner fire. "A great burden has been placed on you, and no one else understands—not like I do."

Razak paced toward the table with his oils, his dreadlocks swaying. He opened the ebony box, revealing the special razor blades he used to create the *barbed warriors*. "If you can help me barber a noble and create the *Tunka Barbed Warrior*, I'll answer your question, pet."

Fanta's expression shifted as she considered his words. She glanced at her scroll, rolling it between her fingers before lifting her lips into a slow, radiant smile. "Then I'll help you right away."

"I hope so... because if we fail, Balansera might fall."

Fanta's eyes flared with determination. "Then let's get to work, my barber. I'm not ready to lose Samba, my family, or my country. And most importantly, I'm not ready to lose you. So, tell me what we need."

Razak smiled, the weight of their situation settling in. "We need to study the records of the past, learn the secrets of the first great barbers. Only then can we understand why I can't confer power to the nobles. If we uncover that, we might still turn this around."

Fanta rose to her feet. "Then it's settled. You keep barbering the warriors for the invasion, and I'll handle the rest. Where can I find this information?"

"Let's start with the archives in the holy temple," Razak replied.

The thunder of elephant horns reverberated across the plains as vast armies marched forward. The alliance of Azemba, Senkoré, and Kelenjara had united their forces at the borders of Senkoré and Balansera—twenty thousand strong. Makan, Jatoba, and Seydou rode side by side, their horses steady beneath them as they surveyed the sheer size of the force before them. Five thousand archers, four thousand cavalry, three thousand infantry armed with heavy maces, five thousand spear-and-shield warriors, and three thousand light infantry wielding javelins. There had been no such host seen in a hundred years.

"Azemba is ready," Makan murmured, his eyes narrowing as he took in the scene. "And so is Senkoré. And Kelenjara..."

Seydou let out a hearty laugh as his horse reared up, its hooves striking the air. "You know we're always ready," he said, his voice light with excitement. "Is there anything else left to say?"

Jatoba, amused, turned his gaze to Seydou. "Is there another word we need to hear?"

A confident smirk spread across Seydou's face as he drew his sword and pointed it toward the golden savannah of Balansera, glistening like a prize ripe for the taking. "Only one..." he said, his voice low and commanding. "Advance!"

Chapter 10

The doors of the throne room crashed open with force, and a guard stumbled through, his eyes wide with alarm. His face was slick with sweat, and he gasped for breath, struggling to regain control of his lungs. The urgency of his entrance was so violent that he collapsed to his knees, still choking for air. The king and his council, who had just completed their war plans, froze, glancing at the guard in shock. Instinctively, several other guards drew their swords and rushed forward.

"Wait!" Balla called, his voice sharp, turning toward the king. "He's not a threat."

The guards hesitated, eyes flicking to the king. With a slight raise of his hand, the king signaled for them to stand down. The warrior, still panting, slowly pushed himself up from the floor.

"Forgive my intrusion, Your Highness," the warrior gasped. "I've ridden from my post on the orders of my lord. The eastern province has been breached. The banners of Azemba, Senkoré, and Kelenjara have crossed our borders."

The room fell into stunned silence. The weight of the news hung in the air.

"Did they cross at different points as separate formations, or are they marching as a single force?" the king asked, his voice controlled but tense.

"They march as one, my king," the warrior replied, his voice still strained.

A murmur spread through the hall. Kandia sat motionless, her face an impassive mask. Balla's fingers tightened around the hilt of his sword, his eyes narrowing as he turned to Samba, who shrugged nonchalantly.

"Alright," the king said, rising from the throne. He began to pace toward the map. "We need to make swift decisions. Our intelligence didn't have time to gather information on their strategy. Do we know who the generals are?"

"Makan, Jatoba, and Seydou lead the force," Balla answered.

"Three generals," the king mused, stroking his beard thoughtfully. "Three formidable generals. But who leads them?"

Balla hesitated, then spoke. "It seems... they are sharing command."

The king absorbed the information for a moment, his gaze distant. "Samba! Gather the entire royal treasury and load it onto carts drawn by the strongest bulls. You'll march straight toward the enemy."

"As you command, Your Majesty." Samba saluted, his voice steady.

"Balla!" the king continued, turning sharply. "Take one hundred of your *Dunfaŋŋo Kulo barbed warriors* and head directly toward the enemy. When you meet them, split your forces—send the treasury north and your warriors south. Make sure your lion roars are heard."

Kandia slowly rose from her seat, her expression unreadable. "My king... cousin... What are you planning?"

The king fixed his gaze on her as he spoke. "I'll march with the main army to the center of their formation. As for the northern and southern forces—do not stop until you've reached the forests on either flank."

Kandia's voice trembled with disbelief. "The whole treasury? You would risk impoverishing the kingdom?"

The king turned to her, his eyes dark with resolve. "We may lose all our wealth today, but we may also survive. This is our only chance."

Back at the military academy, Balla informed Razak of the king's latest decisions, and the Headmaster was visibly taken aback.

"The whole treasury?" Razak raised an eyebrow, his voice tinged with disbelief. "I suppose that includes my salary as well, eh?"

"The livelihood of the entire kingdom," Balla said with a solemn nod. "But the king has faith in us."

Razak's expression hardened as he nodded slowly. "Then my task has just become more urgent. As has Fanta's. But what of the other four hundred *barbed warriors*?"

"They march with the king," Balla replied.

Razak paused, considering the weight of the situation. "So be it. I need to prepare. Kandia's brother will be here soon."

Balla blinked in surprise. "She has a brother?"

"Yes." Razak smiled faintly, his eyes darkening with a hint of mystery. "A secret brother. In fact, he has no official name. But he's the reason I have my tools."

Balla's brow furrowed, a cloud of confusion crossing his features. "What are you planning to do with him?"

Razak turned toward his altar, his voice becoming more reflective. "Ever since I learned about him, I've been... curious. I want to try something. Something different. It seems, my friend, we're all gambling with our futures, hoping that our risks will pay off. The king has made his wager, and now I make mine."

The allied armies crossed the first river at the borders and poured deeper into Balansera. Scouts quickly reported enemy forces approaching their positions, about a week's march away. The generals convened to discuss their next move and decided to take a position on a hill overlooking the plains. The main road ahead split into two directions: one leading north and the other south. After five days of waiting, the force finally came into view.

To their surprise, it appeared that oxen were pulling heavily laden carts, and behind them were one hundred *barbed warriors*.

Makan, Jatoba, and Seydou rode to the top of the hill to witness this sight firsthand. The generals exchanged confused glances.

"What's going on here?" Makan asked, his voice filled with suspicion. "Where is Balansera's army?"

"Perhaps this is just a scouting party, or a small vanguard," Jatoba suggested, shielding his eyes from the harsh sun. "But this doesn't add up."

Seydou's frown deepened. The scene before him was puzzling. He scanned the area beyond the convoy, but no other forces appeared in sight. Without warning, the two groups split at the fork in the road: one heading north, the other south.

"Something's wrong here," Seydou muttered, his mind racing. "They must know we're here by now, yet they're splitting up like this? Why?"

The scouts from the alliance arrived, breathless from their ride.

"My lords!" the foremost scout exclaimed. "The group heading north is Balansera's treasury. It looks like the entire royal treasury."

A stunned silence spread among the three generals, their eyes widening in disbelief.

"And the other group?" Jatoba asked, his curiosity piqued.

"They are five hundred *barbed warriors*, wearing lion-mane styles," the scout replied.

Jatoba's face lit up. "That's it! We capture the treasury, and we've won the war!"

"No!" Seydou interjected, his voice sharp. "This is too easy. They want us to take the bait."

"Who cares?" Jatoba snapped back. "Even if they have ten thousand *barbed warriors*, they won't stop us. The gold is our victory!"

"I agree with Seydou," Makan said, narrowing his eyes at the *barbed warriors* moving south at great speed. "We came here to destroy their magic and their warriors. The gold is a distraction. These *barbed warriors* are the real threat. Prepare to move out. We strike them now."

"Wait!" Seydou called, raising his hand. "This is what they want! Both groups are distractions. We must hold our positions and wait until we know what's really going on. At least until Balansera's main army shows up."

The other two generals exchanged irritated glances but reluctantly nodded in agreement. Yet, it was all in vain. It wasn't long before news spread through the army about the true nature of the slow northern column. Discipline rapidly broke down. Thousands of soldiers began to desert their posts, heading for the gold-laden carts like moths to a flame.

Seydou, alarmed, barked orders to commanders to rein in their troops. But it was too late. The defiant forces, primarily from Jatoba's Senkoré division, charged ahead. Makan, realizing the difficulty of holding the forces back, gave the order for two thousand of his own men to pursue the *barbed warriors* heading south.

Seydou stood at the command post, teeth gritted, as he watched the allied forces splinter into three groups. Within an hour, Senkoré's men reached the caravan. To the south, Makan's men were closing in on the *barbed warriors*.

Suddenly, the air was filled with the sound of arrows. They rained down from nowhere, striking the advancing forces with deadly precision. Panic spread as soldiers scrambled to take cover, but their fear only spurred them to charge forward, driven by the glint of gold from the carts.

But the arrows kept coming—relentless, deadly. The charging soldiers, now nearly blinded by greed, continued forward, ignoring the danger. It was then that the *barbed warriors* revealed themselves. Rising from the grass, they wore intricate hairstyles resembling entwined forest branches. With startling speed, the *barbed warriors* struck, their movements erratic and impossible to track, fading in and out of visibility.

The Senkoré forces who charged were swiftly overwhelmed, falling one by one to the hidden *barbed warriors*, their attacks coming from every angle. The scene was utter chaos, and Seydou, watching from the hill, realized the situation was rapidly spiraling out of control.

Now the only remaining general, Seydou faced a crucial decision. His forces numbered only nine thousand, scattered across three areas. Should he redirect his men to aid Makan's pursuit of the *barbed warriors*, or should he reinforce the caravan and protect the gold?

As he hesitated, war horns sounded in the distance. A new army appeared on the horizon, marching in formation with all their banners and divisions. Seydou could not gauge their strength from this distance. In a flash of clarity, he mounted his horse and ordered his remaining troops to pursue the *barbed warriors* who had gone after the carts.

"Retreat!" Seydou shouted. "Retreat! Retreat!"

It was no use. Few soldiers listened to his commands. The forces were in disarray, and discipline had broken down. Those who obeyed him began retreating back to the hill, but Seydou looked over his shoulder in grim relief as he saw Jatoba's bruised and bloodied form charging toward him, struggling to escape the disaster.

Cissé watched as his forces retreated to their position. The carts continued their journey, guarded by the *Sira Janta barbed warriors* who expertly melded with the vast plains. The first phase of his plan had been a resounding success. That evening, Balla returned, his warriors drenched in blood and dust. He had lost only forty men. In the dense forest, they had successfully repelled Makan's Azemba warriors, whose archers faltered in the uneven terrain and were outpaced by the ferocity of Balla's fighters. Only seven hundred of the enemy had survived their retreat, Makan among them.

"We have tomorrow yet," the king said, his hand firmly resting on Balla's shoulder. He motioned for his warrior to get some rest. Balla nodded weakly and staggered away. "Ah, yes, send me your two most skilled new *barbed warriors*."

Moments later, the two warriors stood before him. The king scrutinized them carefully. One bore the distinctive *Sira Janta* style, while the other wore the unmistakable *Saŋko Fanta* attire. "What are your names?"

"I am Demba, Your Highness."

"And I am Fadiga, King."

The king gave a thoughtful nod. "I have a task for you."

Chapter 11

Deep within the archives of the temple, Fanta pored over ancient scrolls, her search conducted under the watchful gaze of a holy man. Somewhere among these scrolls lay the secrets, inked on pages, detailing the first barber of Balansera. The knowledge she needed to help Razak solve the mystery of barbering the nobles successfully.

The room was filled with towering shelves of scrolls, meticulously organized into categories. Fanta had just finished exploring the history section, which offered detailed accounts of the kingdom's founding. A small village along the banks of the Gambe River had once attracted fishermen and traders. Initially, it served as a resting place for merchants traveling along the Spice Road, which led to Dakumbi—the mighty kingdom at the heart of the world.

While the scrolls provided this information, it wasn't what she sought. Fanta frowned as she replaced the last scroll from the history section. Her mind spun with dates, kingdoms, alliances, marriages, political intrigues, and more.

"I need a break," she muttered, returning to the grand ebony table at the center of the archives. She slumped into a chair and laid her head on the cool surface. "Oh, my barber, this is not what I expected. What am I to do?"

The holy man, who had been quietly watching her from a wall, stepped forward. "My lady, if I could assist you in completing your task, it would allow me to return to mine as well?"

Fanta slowly lifted her head from the table. "In other words, you want to help me so I'm not a bother?"

"Oh, my lady…"

"Is my presence so bothersome?" Fanta sighed. "Even my barber appreciates me more these days."

The holy man stiffened, clearly uncomfortable. "I did not mean to offend. But this task could take all day if I don't help you. You've already been here for hours with no end in sight. Please, allow me to assist."

Fanta smiled faintly, glancing at the table. "Wow, it's been that long? I see. You're right. I can't afford to waste so much time here. There's a war going on, and this information is crucial to the work I'm doing. I must finish it, no matter the cost. I won't fail my barber."

"Your barber?" the holy man asked, raising an eyebrow.

"Oh, yes. You all call him Headmaster."

The holy man's eyes nearly bulged from their sockets. "The Headmaster? Why didn't you say so earlier? Of course, I'll help you!"

Fanta gave him a weary glance. "Is that so? Alright, then. I need information on the first barbers of Balansera."

"Ah, barbers!" The holy man eagerly seized her by the arm, pulling her from the table. "Come with me! You should have told me sooner. Ever since the Headmaster awakened the ancestors' connection to us through his barbering craft, we've been researching all the renowned barbers in the kingdom's history. We've spent months on it. Let me show you!"

Fanta's teeth flashed in a grin as the holy man hurried her along. "You've got me, my holy man. This would have made my life much easier."

Moments later, Fanta was holding five scrolls detailing the first barbers in recorded Balansera history. She devoured the information quickly, but her brow furrowed. She now knew everything about them—but what was the significance? The holy man whispered something in her ear, and Fanta's eyes widened.

"My barber must know immediately!"

I'm surprised you came, Siraŋa." Razak smiled as he welcomed Kandia's secret brother into his chamber at the military academy. A slight twinge of guilt gnawed at him—he only ever engaged with Siraŋa at night.

The young man stood before him, dressed in a simple cloth wrapped around his waist. His sandals were old and dusty, showing the wear of long hours. He was well-built, his physique honed through years of yam production and blacksmithing—both grueling, physical work. His face was strong, with a sharp jawline and light brown eyes, framed by a crown of wild, bushy hair.

Siraŋa glanced around the room. "Does that sister of mine know I'm here?"

Razak shook his head as he gestured to a chair, offering him a seat.

Siraŋa looked at the chair, then back at Razak. "Does she even know I breathe?"

Razak sighed, the weight of the question pressing on him.

Siraŋa's eyes narrowed as he folded his arms across his chest, refusing to sit. "I'm used to plenty of promises going unfulfilled. What am I doing here, Razak? What favor do you want this time?"

"Siraŋa..."

"I never asked for much!" Siraŋa's voice rose with frustration. "You know this, Razak! I don't need recognition, I don't need titles, but at least acknowledge the truth! So, my mother wasn't a noble. So, I'm a bastard. Must my life stay in the shadows?"

Razak bowed his head, unable to meet Siraŋa's gaze. "Please, Siraŋa, I—"

"You promised that you'd look after me. When you discovered the truth. You said you'd speak with them. Yet, you've done nothing. But when you need my help—whether it's with oils or tools—you know I'm there. Always."

Razak raised his head, meeting his gaze. "You're right. You're skilled in so many things, Siraŋa. Blacksmithing among them. That's why I have these special blades." He approached the young man and placed a hand on his shoulder. "You've done everything I've asked, including keeping my secrets. I know you wish for me to act on behalf of your family. But I beg you to be patient."

Siraŋa's eyes gleamed with a hard, searching look as they locked onto Razak's. "So, tell me again... why am I here?"

Razak exhaled slowly, the words heavy on his tongue. "I need you."

Siraŋa jerked away from Razak's hand and turned toward the door, but Razak's voice stopped him.

"Balansera needs you!" Razak called after him.

Siraŋa hesitated at the door, his back still to Razak.

"Please, hear me out." Razak spoke again, motioning to the chair. "Sit with me."

"That's the first time I've heard you say that," Siraŋa remarked over his shoulder, the edge of his voice cutting through the room. "What could Balansera possibly want from me?"

"Your aid."

Siraŋa turned slowly, his shoulders relaxing, a faint shift in his posture as the tension ebbed away. "Balansera's been alright to me. Maybe I'll hear what she has to say."

Razak nodded. "I cannot presume to speak for her, but I will try. And I know I owe you a deep debt concerning the royal family. To Kandia. I know having you return as my apprentice is out of the question."

"You know it is," Siraŋa replied with a short laugh. "But that's not the point. I'm not your first, nor will I be your last. I know that Fanta girl is looking to take my place. Too bad women can't be barbers."

Razak's shoulders sagged. He looked down, defeated. Siraŋa was right. Fanta could not replace him, and Razak still couldn't grant others the power he possessed. But Siraŋa was different. There was something about him—something Razak couldn't quite place. He was the quickest learner, mastering oil blessings in just a few days. His blacksmithing skills had helped Razak create the special blades, which he had then hallowed with care. But Siraŋa's life as a social outcast meant he couldn't advance in society or acquire wealth. His mother lived in constant fear that his true identity would lead to his death—the same fear that had caused Razak to delay the promise he made to his former pupil. But now, with Balansera on the brink of war, Razak had a new premonition about this young man he couldn't shake.

As the sun began its descent, sinking beneath the horizon, men on the opposite side of the capital readied themselves. Clad in dark attire, they helped each other paint their faces, then strapped on their weapons—knives, small axes, and chains with spiked balls. They wrapped dark cloths around their faces, concealing all but their sharp, piercing eyes.

The leader of the group, a seasoned veteran from the Kelenjara army, squatted by the window, catching the last slivers of sunlight to read his orders.

The message was brief:

Our allies are not aligned with our objective concerning the target. Orders are expedited but unchanged. Capture the target alive and return to Kelenjara within twenty-four hours. Failure is unacceptable.

With a heavy sigh, the leader crumpled the letter and tossed it into the hearth, watching the flames devour it slowly. He turned to face his men, who stood in complete silence, their eyes fixed on him. Without a word, he gestured toward the door of their safehouse in the Sunjaro.

The mission had begun.

Razak exhaled slowly, a wave of relief washing over him as Siraŋa eased into the seat Razak had offered.

"Alright, Razak. Will you finally tell me why I'm here?" Siraŋa fixed him with a steady stare.

At that moment, Fanta entered the chamber, pushing open the doors, carrying a single scroll. "I've returned to my barber! I have some important—" She froze when she saw Siraŋa. "Who is this?"

"Ah, she comes herself." Siraŋa smirked. "I must say, she's a bit too pretty for you, Razak."

Fanta glanced at Razak. "My barber?"

"Ah, this is...this is..." Razak faltered.

"Come on, now." Siraŋa chuckled. "Must I remain a secret to this one as well?"

"Yes," Razak muttered.

Fanta raised her hand, gesturing for him to come closer. She leaned in and whispered in his ear.

Razak's face slowly drained of color. "Show me," he whispered urgently.

Fanta handed over the scroll, finding the right section. "Here," she said, pointing to the paragraphs. "The story intrigued me, but does it have any bearing on us?"

Razak absorbed the information. To anyone else, it might seem like just another tale, but he recognized the code. He knew exactly what it meant—and what it could lead to. "My dear pet," he said, his voice low and intense, "I'll drown you in gold if this turns out to be true."

Fanta raised her hands to her chest. "What are you going to do?"

Razak turned to Siraŋa, whose eyes flicked between Razak and Fanta, gleaming with curiosity, tempered by an edge of impatience. "I called you here because I want you to become a *barbed warrior*."

Siraŋa's mouth fell open, and a long silence followed. "Come again?"

"You heard me," Razak said, unwavering.

Siraŋa shook his head, disbelieving. "That's impossible. How? Why?"

"With this." Razak held up the scroll. "I think it might work. After all, you are Kandia's brother."

Fanta gasped, her eyes fixed on Siraŋa, wide with disbelief.

"You can't be serious!" Siraŋa stood abruptly. "I can't even be a *barbed warrior*."

Razak, with surprising force, pulled Siraŋa back into the seat in front of the altar. "You didn't say no. Interesting. But anyway, I'll give it a try."

Siraŋa sat stunned, a wave of confusion washing over him. He was torn between fleeing the room and staying to see where this bizarre conversation would lead. "Even if this works... they'll never accept me. I'm not a noble, I'm a bastard."

Razak moved to his table, retrieving a sleek ebony box. He opened it slowly, taking out one of the razor-sharp blades inside, inspecting it as it caught the torchlight. "Well, society might not see you as a noble, but your blood tells a different story—and that's what matters most."

Razak returned to Siraŋa. "I'm going to make you a *barbed warrior* because Balansera needs you."

Siraŋa smirked, the tension in his posture not quite fading. "It doesn't work on nobles, remember?"

"Well, I think I know why now." Razak said, voice low but sure. "It might work now—but only on someone like you."

"Someone like me? Why?"

"Because you are an outcast." Razak's gaze turned to the altar. "*Baaba ani naana, diyaa ani n'numu banta. Fo n'saniyo la saŋ baŋ ma. Ka kulo ani a fanŋa juŋŋo, fo a banta siraa.*" Ancestors bless the blade, and your son I present to you. Empower his hair as he seeks to serve.

Razak bowed, then approached Siraŋa and began preparing his hair. Fanta resumed her writing in her scroll of accounts.

"What style are you going to try on me?" Siraŋa raised an eyebrow.

Razak smiled faintly. "*Saŋko Fanta* style. Serpent's Coil... *Tunka* level."

Chapter 12

Demba and Fadiga crawled silently along the ground, flanked by a dozen other *barbed warriors*. Their target was the rear of the enemy's army, positioned at the base of the great hill. Demba used his powers to blend into the grass as much as possible, as did the other *barbed warriors* in their group. Fadiga and a few of the Lion Mane-style warriors kept close, careful not to disturb the stealth of their advance. A few hours earlier, the king had given them this mission: to circle behind the enemy. They had moved north, then trekked east, and finally south until they were directly at the enemy's rear. Now, they maneuvered into position, ready to strike.

After another hour of slow, grinding progress, their bodies bruised from the rough crawl, Demba and Fadiga wiped sweat from their eyes. The full outlines of the enemy's encampment came into view, only a few meters away.

"What's the plan now?" Fadiga whispered, his eyes glowing faintly in the dark. His powers allowed him to see clearly in the night.

"What do you see?" Demba whispered back, squinting into the darkness.

Fadiga's eyes scanned the scene. "I see plenty of targets. Looks like the enemy's trying to regroup and recover." His gaze flicked to the northern section of the camp. "I can see their horses tied to the posts."

"Perfect," Demba muttered. "Well, you heard the king. Don't let them sleep too soundly."

Seydou sat motionless, brooding over their losses as he glared at the enemy camp of the Balansera host. Thousands of tents and fires illuminated the chaotic, animated atmosphere below. Moments later, Malan and Jatoba joined him.

"The cursed monsters," Malan growled, his eyes narrowed.

Jatoba sighed and sat beside Seydou, his arm wrapped in a tight bandage. It was clear he was wounded, but the makeshift dressing was enough to keep him in the fight.

"My lords, you've failed to heed my counsel," Seydou snapped, his glare shifting to his counterparts. "We know little of their powers, and yet you charged in anyway."

"Calm down, Seydou," Jatoba responded, his tone measured. "It's not our fault. The enemy set a perfect trap. Once our warriors committed, we had no choice but to follow. I understand your frustration, but this was out of our control."

"General Jatoba is right," Malan added, flicking his knife out with a sharp motion. "Once our warriors charged, they were going to be slaughtered either way. We had no choice but to act quickly and attempt to salvage the situation. The cursed monsters charmed us with their gold. Even I've never seen so much."

Seydou turned his gaze back to the Balansera camp as a cool breeze blew in from the south. It was true they couldn't have predicted the enemy's move with the gold, but the iron discipline of the Kelenjara warriors should have been enough to stop the others from taking the bait.

"What's done is done," Malan said, his voice softening. "Tomorrow we attack in force and destroy these monsters once and for all."

Seydou exchanged a glance with Jatoba, then turned back to Malan. "Maybe we should try my strategy this time." His voice was hard, the weight of command settling on him. "After all, it's my turn to show the enemy what I can do."

Malan frowned, a skeptical look crossing his face. "And what, pray tell, do you think we—"

"Fire!" shouted a nearby guard. "Fire! Fire!" The alarm rang through the camp, spreading like wildfire. The generals sprang to their feet, turning in unison. Horror spread across their faces as chaos erupted around them. Men scrambled to find water to douse the flames, but the fire consumed the dry hides of the tents with terrifying speed. Orders were shouted, but the confusion was overwhelming. The sound of clashing steel soon filled the air.

"Damn fiends!" Jatoba roared, fury in his voice. "This is an attack! Drive them out!" But the smoke and darkness made it hard to see, and Jatoba's voice became drowned in the chaos.

Seydou rallied his bodyguard and charged down the hill, torches in hand, as they navigated through the inferno. Twice, he had to duck to avoid strikes from warriors of their own alliance, who mistook him for the enemy. He knocked them down swiftly, barely breaking stride. He scanned the scene again and again, his sword drawn, ready to strike at any threat— but still nothing.

The night wore on. Slowly, the first light of dawn began to creep over the horizon. A thunderous sound echoed, followed by a deep tremor in the ground. To Seydou's right, the sight that met his eyes was enough to crush the spirit. Several thousand horses stampeded from the camp, and among them, eight riders—Balansera warriors—were galloping westward. They had been attacked again!

Seydou's blood boiled. The enemy had fooled them again. He looked around. Hundreds of his own men lay dead at his feet, slain in the chaos.

"Rally the army!" Seydou bellowed. "Let's send these vermin to hell!"

An hour later, he rejoined the other generals at the top of the hill.

"You're right, Makan," Seydou said, his voice cold with fury. "We still have a numerical advantage, even without the horses. Let's stop playing games. Let's crush them here and now!"

The morning air rang with the thunderous blare of war horns echoing across the field from the enemy camp. The king of Balansera emerged from his tent, clad in royal armor, gilded in gold. The time had come.

"Balla!" The king called, his voice cutting through the rising tension.

"My king!" The barbed general hurried to the king's side.

"Assemble the army for battle." The king's gaze fixed on the hill, which teemed with warriors preparing for the fight. In the distance, closing in on their camp, were the warriors he had sent to stir trouble. "Now that their cavalry is out of the picture, they have no choice but to fight."

Balla gripped his sword hilt, eyes narrowing. "After showing them our power, do you think that's enough to make them retreat and leave us be?"

The king smiled, but it was cold. "We are still young and learning about our powers, while they still see us as nothing more than an upstart. They can't believe what they've seen. Despite all evidence, they refuse to admit it. They will be even more determined to crush us, to prove themselves right."

He turned to Balla. "The enemy still outnumbers us, and we have no more tricks left. Can I still count on you and your warriors?"

Balla saluted, his expression fierce. "You can count on us, to the bitter end."

The king's eyes softened, but his voice remained firm. "May it be sweet, not bitter."

The enemy charged down the hill, a deadly mix of Azemba, Senkoré, and Kelenjara regiments, their weapons gleaming—spears, swords, and shields raised high. Balansera's forces formed three long lines, stretching as far as the eye could see. The king led the center, while Balla commanded the right flank. They waited, ready for the familiar thunderous clash—the enemy's charge crashing into their shields, as it had countless times before.

The enemy closed in with the speed of enraged cheetahs, covering the ground with terrifying swiftness. But then, without warning, the advance halted two hundred yards away. From the enemy's ranks, a volley of arrows soared high, arcing over the field like a deadly storm.

"Shields up!" Balla's voice rang out across the battlefield, filled with urgency. "Shields up!"

The arrows rained down, their deadly tips striking through the air, claiming the lives of hundreds. The shields faltered under the onslaught; they could not withstand the precision of the Azemba bowmen's special arrows, which pierced everything in their range.

Sweat dripped from the king's brow as he stood, faltering. The enemy wasn't charging forward—they were keeping their distance and dealing death from afar. He knew the Kelenjara had provided Azemba armor-piercing steel for their arrows, but he hadn't anticipated such devastating power.

"Balla!" the king called out, but his voice was lost in the chaos. "Samba!"

"My king!" The strong warrior appeared at his side.

The king watched as the enemy continued their relentless assault, volley after volley. The lines were beginning to falter. Several *barbed warriors* had already fallen, their lifeblood staining the ground. This sight alarmed the king. "Samba! We cannot keep going like this. What do you suggest?"

Samba's eyes scanned the enemy ranks. "Pull all the lines back, except for those barbed with the *Jiiya Kuu*, River's Flow style. Like mine," he added, tapping his head.

The king nodded in understanding. "Do it."

Samba moved swiftly, making his way to Balla on the far right of the field. A horn blared across the battlefield, and the Balansera forces began their retreat, pulling back in good order. Another horn sounded, and a hundred *Jiiya Kuu barbed warriors* surged forward, led by Samba.

The enemy's arrows bounced harmlessly away, as if striking invisible water around their shields instead of penetrating them. Samba's warriors had activated their powers, and the deadly barrage lost its effect. Still, the enemy pressed on, releasing volley after volley.

Balla, observing this, hurried back to the king. "My king, I have a plan."

The king raised his hand, signaling his trust. "Whatever you think, Balla, you have my full support. This war began because of the *barbed warriors*. Now it's time for the world to witness the true power Razak has given us. I place the battle in your hands."

"Your highness!" Balla saluted once more. He turned and rushed back to the field, where he found Samba. "Your warriors will join with mine. We'll fight as one and break them."

"Let's drive them out, for good," Samba smirked, his eyes alight with resolve.

The Balansera army reformed with a new formation. *Jiiya Kuu barbed warriors* were interspersed throughout the ranks, their powers still deflecting the arrows that rained down from the enemy. When the formation was ready, Balla drew his sword, his voice rising to rally the troops.

"This is our moment, warriors of Balansera!" he shouted, his words shaking the air. "We may not have the numbers to crush them, but we are all the kingdom has left. Many of us were ordinary men before we were called to serve, to protect. The Headmaster entrusted us with powers to connect with our ancestors, to shield our people. If we fail today, we fail not only them but the ancestors who believed in us. We cannot fail! Trust in your powers. Trust in your brothers—they will protect your back. Let this be the moment the griots sing of our deeds. Rise now! To battle! Into history, into the future!"

A great roar rose from the Balansera ranks, shaking the very ground beneath their feet. The enemy, now disarmed of their bows, took up their spears and swords in desperate defense. At that moment, the *Dunfaŋŋo Kulo barbed warriors* howled, activating their lion powers, filling the battlefield with fear before charging into the enemy lines. The other *barbed warriors* followed, cutting down their foes with brutal force, their strikes shattering armor and bringing death in their wake.

The battle swayed as both sides threw in their final reserves. Then, suddenly, a thunderous crack split the air. At the rear of the Balansera lines, the *Suŋkaani Fatta barbed warriors* raised their hands to the sky. Fifty of them shone with blue light, their energy surging like a storm. With a mighty gesture, they unleashed a torrent of lightning, raining death upon the enemy, frying them where they stood. The enemy's formations splintered apart like torn cloth, and they began to flee the battlefield. The Balansera warriors gave chase, striking down the remnants of the retreating force with unrelenting fury, their battle cry still echoing like a fire that could not be quenched.

An hour later, the king stood on the hill that had once been the enemy alliance's campsite, his gaze sweeping across the scene before him. Thousands of fallen foes lay scattered across the battlefield—dead or dying. Balla and Samba flanked him, both silent as they surveyed their hard-won victory.

"This victory is yours, Balla, and yours, Samba," the king said, his voice low with reverence. "Without you and your *barbed warriors*, our history would have ended today. But now..." He turned his gaze eastward, the weight of the moment settling over him. "Our history begins a new chapter."

"As long as we have the Magic Barber," Balla said with a grin. "Our nation's story will grow ever stronger."

Samba's lips curled into a smirk. "About time, too."

Chapter 13

Razak poured all his energy into his craft, his hand steady as he completed the final etching of the coil on the left side of Siraŋa's head. With a practiced motion, he took a small comb and inserted it near the top of the head, gently pushing the bushy hair back into place. Fanta, seated in the corner, paused in her writing, her eyes fixed on Razak's meticulous work.

"This is different," she remarked, her tone thoughtful. "You usually keep the hair low on top. But now you're holding it in place with the comb. Are you planning to keep it bushy on top?"

"Very perceptive, pet," Razak replied, stepping back to gain a better view of his work. "This isn't the usual *Saŋko Fanta* style. It's a more complex design, requiring elements that won't be found in standard styles."

Siraŋa raised an eyebrow in silent curiosity.

"*Tunka...* must be something special," Fanta mused as she returned to her records. "How many will you be able to do?"

Razak paused, the blade hovering in the air as he sighed. That was the question, wasn't it? If this worked, he would have a clearer idea of the criteria for selecting potential candidates. But even then, it was rare—finding them would be a struggle. "First, we need to see if this works. If not... we're back at the beginning."

Fanta nodded, her expression thoughtful. "And how do you think the king's plan will unfold?"

"The king's plan is daring, to say the least," Razak said, his voice filled with quiet respect. "He's been a brilliant strategist throughout his life. It's thanks to him that the kingdom has endured this long. But despite his brilliance, we've never been strong. Not until now. The emergence of the *barbed warriors* will change everything. The Balansera kingdom will become a nation to be reckoned with. A center of barbering craft. Our work will be legendary."

Fanta's voice was soft, but filled with sincerity. "Well, I'm happy for you."

Razak glanced at her, surprised.

"I'll take everything you've taught me and apply it to our ladies," she said with a smile. "You've taught me so much, not just for my future husband, but for my own path. Watching you work has inspired me to pursue the art of hair. I want to open my own beauty salon and become the best hairstylist."

Razak's eyes widened, his gaze shifting back to Sirana as he absorbed her words. The etching was now complete, and the design's frontal lineup was set. He turned his focus to the hair on top. "I would gladly support your venture. I'm intrigued to see what you'll create. The sacred art of hair is not reserved for men alone."

Fanta's smile deepened. "Thank you, my barber."

Razak returned the smile as he took the loose hair held by the comb, beginning to braid it with practiced hands. The strands flowed smoothly, weaving together to cascade on both sides of Siraŋa's head and towards the back. "My pet, I thirst. Please fetch me some calabashes of water."

Fanta glanced up, her gaze soft. "Yes, my barber."

Fanta exited the chamber and stepped into the cool night air of the courtyard. She paused, taking a deep breath as the breeze brushed against her skin. Only the starlight and the flickering torches mounted on the walls illuminated the path ahead. She walked along the pillared courtyard, making her way to the well at the northern end near the gates. Guards patrolled the walls and the gates, at least one hundred of them, as the majority of the academy's forces were mobilized for the frontlines.

Approaching an elderly man tending to the well, Fanta spoke softly, "Two calabashes for the Headmaster, please."

The old man nodded and began working the pulley system, drawing water from deep below in small jars that would empty into the waiting calabashes.

Crack.

Fanta flinched at the sound, instinctively turning her head. A breeze stirred through her braids, and a sudden chill crept up her spine. She glanced around, but nothing seemed out of place. The gates remained manned by a few guards, and others were stationed along the walls. Yet the eerie feeling didn't subside.

"For the Headmaster," the old man called, motioning toward the filled calabashes.

"Thank you," Fanta said, forcing a smile as she took them. She turned and began walking slowly back through the courtyard. A torch flickered along the wall, causing her to spin sharply. But the flame steadied, burning brightly as it always had. She blinked, scanning the shadows—nothing seemed amiss. *Was that a shadow?* She wondered, blinking again. She exhaled, her unease deepening. "I need to get out of here. Tonight feels off."

Picking up her pace, she slid her slippers against the stone, the soft sound of her shuffling footsteps the only noise around her.

Bam!

A sudden crash echoed across the courtyard, startling Fanta so violently that she nearly cried out. A large bundle lay in the distance, just out of the torchlight's reach. She set the calabashes down and crept toward it, pulling at the bundle with trembling hands. It was heavy, and wet—stained with something red. With a final, desperate tug, she managed to flip it over.

It was one of the guards.

Dead.

A scream tore from her throat, raw and filled with dread. Her gaze shot upward, and she saw shadows shifting across the rooftops of the academy walls. One shadow leapt down. Without thinking, she grabbed the calabashes, threw the water at the figure's face, and fled.

The sound of her scream triggered a general alarm. Guards rushed to her position, but the shadows were already upon them. Figures clad in black emerged from the darkness, brandishing short weapons. They hurled knives, their targets falling instantly, while others swung axes, cutting down the guards.

Fanta sprinted across the courtyard, heart pounding, as the battle escalated. Roars of battle filled the air, and the clash of steel against flesh rang out. The guards fought valiantly, but they were outmatched. More shadows dropped into the courtyard, surrounding the defenders and overwhelming them.

Leaning against a pillar on the south side of the courtyard, Fanta tried to catch her breath. The chaos was horrifying. The battle was bloody, ferocious. Guards fell one after another, and the air was thick with the stench of blood. Who were these invaders? What did they want?

The dreadful realization struck her like a bolt of lightning.

"They're here for my barber!"

Her heart raced. She quickly slipped off her slippers, moving as quietly as possible along the pillared wall. She took the long route back to the Headmaster's chamber, where four guards stood watch.

"Lady Fanta!" one of them called, raising a hand. "Get inside! You need to get the Headmaster to safety! They're after him! Protect him, make sure he escapes!"

Fanta nodded, her hands shaking as she grabbed the door handle and yanked it open. She darted inside, moving quickly through the darkened corridors. She didn't stop until she reached the ebony doors of Razak's chambers. Without hesitation, she burst in and slammed the door shut behind her, bolting it with trembling hands.

Razak stared at Fanta, his expression slowly morphing from focus to shock. She was drenched in sweat, her chest rising and falling rapidly. Something had happened—something serious. He was still in the midst of braiding Sirana's hair, carefully intertwining wire gold into the strands. There was more work to do, but now... his attention was entirely on Fanta.

Sirana's head turned in her direction. "Fanta, what's going on?"

Fanta gasped for breath, her voice strained as she tried to speak. "My barber... my barb... flee!"

Razak's eyes widened as he rushed toward her. "Are you alright, Fanta?"

"I'm fine, my barber," she panted, "But I won't be if they catch you!"

The distant crash of the academy's doors echoed through the hall. The sound of steel clashing and the dying screams that followed left no doubt: *they were here.*

"They've come for us," Razak muttered, his voice dark with realization.

"They've come for you," Fanta corrected, her voice trembling with urgency. "They know! The nations know. Somehow, they know about you. You have to escape!"

Razak frowned, his face hardening with resolve. "There's nowhere to run, my pet."

Tears welled in Fanta's eyes as she swallowed hard. "What are you going to do, my barber?"

Another violent crash, followed by the thunderous rumble of stampeding feet, shook the chamber.

Bam!

The intruders rammed into the ebony doors with all their strength, shaking the walls of the room.

Razak turned back to Siraŋa, whose face was grim, but whose eyes blazed with determination. "I'll do what I know. What I can. Barber."

He quickly resumed his work, braiding the final strands of Siraŋa's hair, weaving gold wire with deft fingers.

"How much time do we have?" Siraŋa asked, his eyes locked on the ebony door, now groaning under the battering force.

"Ebony is strong," Razak replied, his fingers moving faster, "But only the ancestors know how long it will hold."

Fanta, trembling, dropped to her knees at the altar and began praying fervently.

"Even if you finish and it works, what do I do?" Siraŋa's voice was tight with uncertainty. "How do I wield this power?"

Razak mumbled through gritted teeth, his fingers flying with practiced speed. "Worry not, my friend."

Crunch!

A hole appeared in the door, and a glaring eye peeked through. It locked onto Siraŋa, then Razak. The eye disappeared, and voices in Kelenjara rattled off before the ramming continued.

"Open your mind and your heart," Razak said as he worked on the final braid. "Then you will know what to do."

Sirana's eyes narrowed, determination settling on his features.

Bam!

More pieces of the door splintered and crashed to the ground. Fanta's prayers grew louder, her voice shaking with intensity. Sweat dripped from Razak's brow, and the rhythmic weaving of his hands became his only focus. His body was drenched, his fingers slipping with the sweat of his exertion as time seemed to slow.

The final braid... it was almost done.

BAM!

The doors shattered completely, collapsing in a thunderous crash.

Razak snipped the excess wire from the last braid just as a dozen intruders burst into the chamber. Fanta threw herself in front of him, her teary eyes now blazing with defiance. Razak's arms went around her, holding her close as he glared at the invaders.

Sirana's eyes began to glow green, and the intruders froze, their eyes wide with terror. Then, his eyes blazed with golden fire, and a fierce wind swirled around him, enveloping him in a golden aura like flames.

Sirana slowly rose from his seat, the power radiating off him in waves.

The intruders gasped. "He's a *barbed warrior*! Kill him!"

Sirana moved like a blur. He struck out with lightning speed, knocking warriors down one by one, leaving them paralyzed. Three blades slashed toward him, but he dodged them effortlessly. A quick kick sent one warrior crashing into the wall, and Sirana rolled to grab a sword from the floor.

Power surged through him, taking the shape of fiery coils around his arm as he wielded the blade.

Five more warriors charged, but it was like they were moving in slow motion. Siraŋa parried every blow with ease, his sword cutting through flesh and bone with terrifying precision. Blood dripped from the blade as the warriors fell to the ground, gasping for breath as venom from the poisoned sword coursed through their veins.

The remaining warriors, clearly intimidated, surrounded him. The leader, a towering figure, pointed his sword at Siraŋa and barked orders in Kelenjara.

"It's over!" The leader roared.

He turned to Razak. "Time to go, Magic Barber."

Siraŋa's lips curled into a smirk as his eyes glowed once more with golden energy. With a single raised arm, a surge of power ripped through the room. Giant flaming coils materialized, wrapping around the remaining five warriors who were within fifteen feet of him.

Razak and Fanta gasped in awe. This... this was another level of power—*the power of a Tunka Barbed Warrior.*

The fiery coils pulled the warriors toward Siraŋa, arranging them in a neat row before him. Fear and shock painted their faces as they realized they were completely at his mercy.

Siraŋa clenched his fist, and the coils tightened, slowly crushing the warriors with horrifying precision. Earsplitting screams filled the room as bones cracked and bodies were squeezed of their life force.

It was over.

With a final release, Siraŋa dropped his arm. The lifeless forms of the attackers fell to the ground in a heap.

Siraŋa collapsed, spent, his body trembling from the sheer exertion. Fanta rushed to his side, her hands shaking as she dabbed the sweat from his brow.

"Siraŋa!" she cried. "Are you alright? Are you okay?"

He smiled faintly, his voice weak. "I'm alright... just... exhausted." His eyes flicked to Razak. "You were right. Once I let go... I knew what to do."

Razak nodded, his wide eyes reflecting something between awe and fear.

Fanta turned to him, her voice filled with wonder. "My barber, I've never seen power like this before. What just happened? What have we discovered?"

Razak's lips curled into a slow smile, his gaze fixed on Siraŋa. "We've discovered the next chapter in the history of barbering."

Acknowledgements

I would like to first and foremost thank God for making this possible. I also thank my mother, Bisi Adjapon, who sparked my love for reading and storytelling back in elementary school.

A heartfelt thanks to my beta readers, Marie Francoise and Gion Karlo, for their invaluable feedback in helping shape this story. And last but certainly not least, my barber Razak, whose skill and spirit inspired this book.

Author's Note

My barber, knowing the work I've done in Fantasy and Historical Fiction, once told me he wished I'd write a story featuring him. So I did.

As I developed this tale, I decided to place his character in a magical setting inspired by a historical period—roughly five hundred years before the rise of the Ghana Empire in West Africa. The lands and kingdoms of Balansera, Azemba, Senkoré, Kelenjara, and Dakumbi are entirely fictional, though they are grounded in the spirit of pre-imperial West African civilization.

The geography in the story is intentionally lush and fertile, drawing from the theory that the Sahara was once a green and thriving region during earlier climatic periods.

The barbering techniques and magic described in the book were created in collaboration with my own barber, Razak, whose skill and creativity helped shape the heart of this story.

About the Author

Tolu Adjapon is a U.S.-born Ghanaian author with a passion for African-inspired fantasy and historical storytelling. He also works professionally in international trade and business sustainability.

When he's not writing, Tolu enjoys reading, watching sports, and spending time with friends and family. The Magic Barber is his debut novella, blending cultural tradition with imaginative world-building.